Kissing Annabel

Love, Ghosts, & Facial Hair and *A Place Like This*

Kissing *Annabel*

Love, Ghosts, & Facial Hair and *A Place Like This*

Steven Herrick

SIMON PULSE
New York   London   Toronto   Sydney

SIMON PULSE

An imprint of Simon & Schuster Children's Publishing Division

1230 Avenue of the Americas, New York, NY 10020

Love, Ghosts & Facial Hair copyright © 1996 by Steven Herrick

A Place Like This copyright © 1998 by Steven Herrick

These titles were originally published individually in Australia by the University of Queensland Press.

All rights reserved, including the right of reproduction in whole or in part in any form.

SIMON PULSE and colophon are registered trademarks of Simon & Schuster, Inc.

The text of this book was set in Berthold Akzidenz and Bernhard Modern.

Manufactured in the United States of America

This Simon Pulse edition January 2009

2 4 6 8 10 9 7 5 3 1

Library of Congress Control Numbers:

Love, Ghosts & Facial Hair: 2003110835

A Place Like This: 2003110836

ISBN-13: 978-1-4169-8287-6

ISBN-10: 1-4169-8287-6

Love, Ghosts & Facial Hair

Dedicated to the backyard cricket pitch at Katoomba

CONTENTS

my family

there's a ghost in our house

the wild orchard

making a living

echoes

My Family

My name is Jack
not Jackson
or Jackie
not Jack-in-the-box
    laughing like an echo
not hit the road Jack
not Jack the rat
or Jack, go wash your face
or Jack rabbit
    lifting my head to get shot
or Jacqueline
not Jack of all trades
    master of none
or car Jack
or Jack Frost
not Jackpot
    the name of a loser

or Jackboot
or Jacktar
or Jackknife
or Jacket
    something to wrap yourself in
not just Jack
or Jack of hearts
but
JACK

OK?

*M*y family (the dream one)

There's my Dad
dressed in his best blue suit
counting his money ($10,000, $11,000, $12,000 ...)
My Mum
she'll be home soon
she's starring in another movie
so she's acting late.
And my sister? she's away.
She's a Nun, helping the poor in Africa
they had her on *60 Minutes* last week
Saint Sister they call her.
My brother?
he's outside polishing his Porsche.
And me
I'm just starting my maths homework.
I love maths.

My family (the real one)

There's my Dad
snoring in his chair, still in his work clothes
sleeping without a shower for the third day running.
My Mum
she's wearing those pink curlers in her hair
looks like a Space Cadet to me.
And my sister's in the bathroom
she's dyeing her hair orange
I think it'll suit her.
My brother?
he's in jail, we expect him home next year.
And I'm here writing this, watching the footy on TV
and doing everything possible to avoid
homework.

My family (the truth)

Actually, truth be known
they're both wrong.
I live with my Dad
and my sister.
My Dad works at a newspaper
he says he tells "edited lies" all day
he's a journalist
which means I never see him.
He leaves home at 7am
and returns at night
smelling of cigarette smoke and defeat.
He walks in
reheats the dinner
and asks me if I've done my homework.
He's OK though.
He talks to me on the weekends
and that's enough for a parent.
My sister I like!
yeah I know
you're not supposed to like your sister
but Desiree's great.

She left school last year
went right out and got a job.
She's Assistant Manager of a bookshop.
She says they'll stock my first book
when it's published.
She's nineteen.
Tall, dark eyes, long black hair,
and
this faint trace of soft light hair on her top lip!
that's what I like about her
she's upfront
other girls might wax it
but not Des
I tell her it looks sexy
and I think it does (for my sister!)
so Des & me
get on fine
she even talks to me
about Ms Curling
and Annabel Browning.

Sex, sport, & nose hair

I'm a normal guy.
An average sixteen-year-old.
I think about sex, sport, & nose hair.
Sex mostly.
How to do it
how to get someone to do it with me
who I should ask for advice.
My friends are useless
they know nothing.
We sit, at lunchtime,
trying to make sense of that
impenetrable mystery called girls.
I've thought of asking Ms Curling
she's the type who'd look me in the eye
and talk straight
but I could never hold her stare
I'd start dribbling, or blushing, or coughing
or worse

I'd get an erection!
they happen at the worst times.
In the bus
In Science class
I spent all Friday night thinking I must be
perverted to get excited during Science!
so, I can't ask my teachers, or friends,
Dad?
it's so long since he had sex
he'd have trouble remembering.
I'd be better asking him
about nose hair!

Desiree!
She'll tell me …

Desiree on sex

"Des, I want to know about sex."

    "Like what?"

"Like how, why, when, & who with."

    "How is simple. Hands, lips
    kissing, touching.
    Why? Because it feels good
    and costs nothing, except
    for the condom.
    When? When Dad's not home.
    Or on the weekend, somewhere nice,
    like the hut near Megalong Creek.
    Who with? Can't help you, sorry.
    Why not ask Annabel Browning on a date?
    You keep talking about her ..."

Trust Desiree to answer
everything about sex in about fifty words
and bring up Annabel Browning.

Another poem on sex, sport, & nose hair

Sex is late-night games on the computer
    thinking "there must be better things to do".
Sex is the morning newspaper crimes
    with my Dad shaking his head
    saying "what a world, what a world".
Sex is with a condom
    or so the school counsellor says.
Sex is the beach in summer
    the smell of suntan oil
    the long train ride home, alone,
    reading a book.
Sex is acne, greasy hair, and shopping
    for the Hollywood gloss of magazines
    and movies.
Sport is as much energy as sex
    yet half the fun, I imagine.
Sport is the only time
    you'd get me wrapping my arms
    around Peter Blake's legs!
Sport is the way we decide who should
    be the School Captain.
Sport is money, broken noses, & played
    by guys with thick necks!
Nose hair is my destiny.
Nose hair will prevent me from having sex
    until I'm too old to care.
Nose hair is the first thing I check in the morning.
Nose hair bristles in the afternoon wind.
Nose hair keeps my mind off girls, maths,
    and the adventure of sleeping.

A writer

I'm going to be a writer
I decided yesterday
while Ms Curling, my Art teacher,
had my head cradled in her arms,
wiping my brow
with a warm towel.
We were surrounded by
twenty-one fellow students, all in football gear,
and two less-concerned teachers.
It seems my face and someone's elbow
had a close encounter.
the result, Ms Curling's *Chanel #5*
wafting through
my newly-broken nose.
Maybe it was this,
and her concerned caress,
or the thought
of another fifteen games
left in the season
that decided it ...

yes
I'm going to be a writer
beat the typewriter
not my mates
no more change-room jokes on muscles
or competitions for the smelliest socks.
I'm retiring
joining the guys on the outer.
I'm going to wear dark clothes
and an intense expression.

If nothing else
I hope it will attract the girls.

The great poem

I have just written a great poem.
A Classic.
One that's so good
University Professors will read it, badly,
in front of hundreds of students
twenty years
         after I die
to prove to the world
what a jewel
what a gift
what a gem
         I gave
what a poet I was.
Here in my Blue Mountains garret
I light another imaginary cigarette
                  to celebrate
death and the poem.
I'm sending it to every publisher in the land
I want them to fight for it
I'm sitting at my desk trying to choose the pen
I'll use to sign the contracts
         to sign the Movie Rights
I'm sorry it's night, or I'd ring the Chat Shows
to arrange to read it live to the Nation!
Ms Curling, my Dad, Desiree
will shake their heads in disbelief.
  A great poem from "what's his name" …

*L*ove is like a gobstopper

Love is like a gobstopper
it's true
you spend all your childhood
wanting that perfect round life-giving
never-ending ball of sweetness
you look through the shop window
    your mouth waters
    legs shake
    eyes go in and out of focus
until that desired gobstopper is yours.
    You hold it
    cherish it
    kiss it
    dream about it
sleep with it under your pillow
wake up sticky
and hope you'll never be alone
but like all lovers
you want more
so one tempting night
you close your eyes
push it all the way into your mouth
and taste its wonder
    then you swallow it
    choke
    and die!
Love is like a gobstopper.

Desiree on facial hair

It's Jack who's to blame
his obsession with facial hair
has got me looking at my moustache
God! he's even got me calling it that
when it's only light lip hair
and now I can't look at anyone
without noticing the shadow above their mouth.
Three weeks of research has proven
that every woman I know has facial hair.
The only people without it seem to be
models and movie stars
and we all know about their grip on reality!
so I'm keeping mine
despite my hairdresser
mentioning it every time I see her.
Waxing, electrolysis, dyeing —
give me a break.
And besides, I'm beginning to like it
maybe Jack is right
maybe it is sexy
let's face it
it's certainly more attractive than nose hair.

Violence in the Family

Today I'm going to watch my Dad
    hit a white ball with a big silver stick
when he's hit the ball
he's going to walk after it
    carrying a whole bag of big sticks
when he finds the ball, hiding, grass-stained
he's going to hit it again
    until it does what it's told
    and falls in the hole.
Sometimes it refuses
    and he bashes the big stick
    on the ground in threat
occasionally he drowns the ball in a lake
    and walks silently away
once he stamped his petulant feet
    quickly looked around
    alone, and ashamed
    and gave the little ball an almighty smack.
After doing this for a few hours
    he'll put the ball and sticks in the car
    drive home
    and boast about his game to me and Des.
One day he asked Desiree to join him
    but she smiled no
    as she took a knife from the drawer
    went to the fridge
    dragged an onion out
    and slowly, deliberately
    cut its head off.

There's a Ghost in Our House

_C_ ancer

They said it was a harmless lump
    it wasn't
they said the signs were good
    they weren't
they said she needed tests
    we all did
they said they found it too late
    no, too early
they said she had six months
    she didn't
they said the pills eased the pain
    they only gave them to Mum
they said Dad was being strong
    he wasn't
they said Desiree and I didn't understand
    we did
they said it was hereditary
    now Dad calls the doctor if I get a headache
they said the hospital room smelt fresh
    it smelt of death
they said the funeral was stirring
we came home alone.

Don't believe

Don't believe in leaders
don't believe anyone who calls you mate
    twice in one sentence
don't believe in people who always do what's right
don't believe in people with religious placards
    who stop you in the street and say
    "this will only take five minutes of your time"
don't believe in tax cuts
don't believe anyone who parts their hair in the middle
don't believe what you read, unless I wrote it
don't believe stallholders at community markets
    who say "yes, of course it's handcrafted"
don't believe school counsellors
    who say they can help you
don't believe in money, unless you've got some
don't believe in pop stars with runny noses
don't believe pop stars anyway
don't believe teachers
    they really want to dress like that
don't believe anyone who votes Liberal
don't believe anyone who votes National
    BELIEVE anyone who votes Labor
    no one that stupid could lie
don't believe anyone who owns a Barry Manilow CD
don't believe anyone who owns a Guns & Roses CD
to be safe, don't believe anyone who owns a CD player
and never, but never, believe doctors who say
"everything will be all right".

The photo

It's the only photo I carry
the four of us
Dad with his arm around Mum's waist
both standing in the holiday fresh water
Desiree and me pushing into the frame
I'm pointing at Dad's arm
I'd never seen them stand that close
Desiree is looking straight at the camera
    her chest out
       the pride of a one-piece swimsuit
       at thirteen, sunning in the attention.

After the photo Mum and Dad
    lie on the sand
    they hold hands
I keep kicking the ball their way
    like a troublesome dog with a stick
    no one wants to throw.
Desiree is off talking to boys
I kick the ball for the return of the waves
and count how many times Mum and Dad kiss.

Seven years ago
on the beach
Mum and Dad
kissed
twenty-four times
and never once
saw anyone else
or thought of anyone else.

Twenty-four times.

It's the only photo I carry
it's in my wallet.

The family holiday

I remember that last holiday with my wife,
Jack and Desiree.
Fish and chips, with no dishes to wash
teaching Jack to bodysurf
sand in our shorts
Desiree talking to the boys at the shops
      looking to see if we could hear
ice-cream for dessert
kissing my wife on the beach
the orange evening sky
walking from headland to lighthouse
Jack kicking the ball at seagulls
the rain that only fell at night
      and cleared to summer at six am.
The distant hum of Saturday sport
everyone nodding "hello" down the main street
Desiree and Jack sleeping till late
my wife, my wife
talking to me
      and I'm drinking it in.

There's a ghost in our house

There's a ghost in our house
in a red evening dress
black stockings
    and Mum's slingback shoes
her hair whispers
    over white shoulders
as she dances through the rooms.
In Desiree's
    she cleans under the bed
folds the five pairs of Levi's
Des wears for months without washing.
In my room
    she flips through my poems
to the one about Mum & Dad at the beach
    the poem glows as I sleep.
In Dad's room
    she sits at the dresser
I can see her
    smiling at the mirror too scared
to announce her presence.

Once, when I stood to watch
    she winked
like an over-excited schoolgirl
    the ghost winked at me.
Annabel Browning
Ms Curling
and whatever future I'd planned
disappeared
in that moment of me and the ghost
    playing hide & seek
breathing
    in the shadow of history
retying a cord
    that should never have been cut.

There's a ghost in our house
in Mum's
red evening dress.

Shoes, socks, the lock on the bathroom door

When I think of our house
I think of shoes
socks
and the lock on the bathroom door.
Dad's golf shoes on the washing machine
Desiree's work shoes on her wardrobe
her Baxter boots flung over the lounge
        with the rest of her attached.
Dad's socks, as he walks to the bathroom
Dad's socks, soaking in the sink
Desiree's stockings hanging from the shower rail
        the run in her black ones.
My football boots, shiny, worn once
        in the garbage
my Doc's with the toe pushing through
Dad's brown shoes
        "brown shoes, brown personality" Desiree says.
Desiree's baby booties tied to her mirror
        pink, with pink bows, my Mum's handiwork.
My socks, the ones with Batman on them
        Dad's idea of cool!
my football socks, full of spare change
        sagging from a hook on the wall.

The lock on the bathroom door
    when my Dad reads the paper.
    Desiree every morning in a rush.
    Me, when I eat too much
    or when I want to write and the TV's on
where I'm sitting now
in the bath, writing this,
thinking one day, to please Dad
I'm going to have to wear
those bloody Batman socks!

Coooeee

Me and Dad
have nothing to do this Saturday
so we go for a walk
through the bush
to our favourite spot
"Jack's Lookout"
Dad named it
on our first visit
with Mum and Desiree
when I was five.
It's a granite rock
high above Megalong Valley
and on a sunny day
you can see forever.

I loved it there
the parrots chimed through the gums
a stream rippled below
and I think of our first visit
the picnic lunch
and Dad, hands cupped, shouting
"Coooooeeeee"
across the cliffs
their echo sounding once each
for the four of us.

At five years old, I thought Dad
was shouting
"do a wee"
and kept asking him
for one more echo
A grown man telling the world
about his toilet habits
and his kids rolling on the rock
saying
"One more Dad, one more"
and him, never understanding
why we laughed the whole weekend.

I'm sixteen now,
I'm trying to decide
as we walk this bush track
whether to ask my Dad
to shout once more
and tell him about it
or keep a secret
between Des, and Mum, and me,
and the family history.

Dad writes poetry

Jack, when I was sixteen
I wanted to play football every day
until I was old, thirty-five, or forty.
And at forty
I wanted to buy a house on a cliff
wander to the beach
make love in the sand
then come home and drink all afternoon.
This seemed a good plan for my life.
My teacher said I was being unrealistic
my Mother said I was being stupid
my Dad said I wasn't that good at football
and my girlfriend didn't say anything
        because I didn't have one.
So at sixteen
I set off on my plan.
The first game of football
        I broke my arm
the first time at the beach
        I nearly drowned
the first time I drank lots of beer
        I puked
and the first time I made love
        I'd rather not say.
So I gave up football
        and swimming

although I still occasionally practise drinking
and alone at fifty
    making love is not such an issue
    although everyone says it should be.
So Jack, when I look back
the only thing that was worthwhile,
apart from having you and Desiree
and falling in love with your Mum,
    was writing poetry.
At sixteen I thought poems were for old people
and always about flowers, or death,
or "ducks gliding gracefully across the millpond"
but the only ducks I saw
    were in Chinese take-away shops
so I guess I have learnt something
    even if it's taken me
                half my life.

The family team

We wanted more children
I planned a football team
Desiree's kick in your Mother's stomach
    held promise
    a backyard of winners
we had a long list of names
    ready, in the top drawer
we saved your baby clothes
we planned extra bedrooms
we promised your Grandma
    (she held on for years)
we had dreams of a farm
we'd welcome each year with a child
we'd fill the one-teacher-school with our own
I was going to learn to milk a cow
                drive a tractor
                change a nappy
                all at the same time!
we would never grow old
    with so many children

but the cancer ripped our family
and this heart
    that now only pumps blood

we wanted more children
we would never grow old
now
I want more children
and your Mother will never grow old.

The cubbyhouse

Dad's thinking of knocking down the cubbyhouse.
It sits, weed lonely at the bottom of the yard
home of rusted toys
    rain-soaked curtains
and my initials carved inside the door.
Dad says he could use the space
    and the wood.
The last time any of us went inside
was the night Des and I got locked out
and needed somewhere to wait.

So Dad and I
    hammer, saw, crowbar,
circle the cubbyhouse
    neither wanting to swing the first blow
and I check inside for my initials
and show Dad
and he fingers the hinge of the door
and smells the scent of old timber
and gets that faraway look in his eyes
as he tells me how
    he built this
the day of the 1986 Grand Final
    Dad in the backyard hammering nails
    as Parramatta hammered Canterbury

and he tells me that
Des and I climbed in
as soon as the floor was up
and we didn't leave till dark
and every night for two weeks
Mum had to bring dinner down here
and once, in summer,
Des and I, and Dad,
slept here all night
     and told stories to the wind.

Dad and I pick up the tools
and put them back in the shed.
Dad takes one look at the untouched cubby
and says he's heading into town
to the hardware
     for some paint.

Wine

He drinks red wine during the week
one glass at dinner
another for dessert
    he pats his stomach
    smiles, with perfect teeth
and tells us
    he's fighting ulcers and a heart condition
    the best way he knows.
Desiree says
    at least red wine doesn't smell,
    not like the bottle of Riesling
    he drinks for Saturday lunch
and afterwards
    he tries to interest me
    in a game of cricket.
At sixteen years of age
    I realise how regular
    adults need humouring
Desiree tells him to act his age
Dad and I ignore her
    as I tap the cricket bat
    in front of the stumps
and Dad walks back to his mark
    a glass in one hand
    ball in the other
and for the past five years
I've watched him bowl his gangly
leg-spin
and never once
    spill a drop.

Signature

Ezra is my friend
he's finishing school soon
    moving straight to work
    and his father's designs.
I'll miss him
we sit against the fence
he takes a poem he's written
    out of the sling for his broken arm
I read it
    his parents arguing down the page.
Ezra looks across the oval
tapping his fingers
on the plaster cast
I can see the poem hurt more than the arm
he's waiting for me
    to lie
    or tear it up
    or tell him to change the last line.
And I can't help thinking
that the poem and the arm
happened in the same place
and which came first
which will last longer
and then I know what to do
    I give him back the poem
    smile
and ask if I can sign my name
on his plaster cast.

Katoomba

This is the only school assignment I've enjoyed.
I've been looking through a book of
Aboriginal Place Names
for a study of our suburb
whose name means
"place where waters tumble over hill"
now this may have been accurate before 1813
but today I'd say it's either
"place where Japanese tourists tumble over hill"
or
"place where polluted water stagnates".
If I had a choice I'd call it
Cobba-da-mana
meaning "caught by the head"
and I know a few Year 9s that name suits perfectly.
Or this one, in honour of our
Physical Education teacher:
Barnawather ... "deaf and dumb"
or Desiree's favourite:
Pugonda, meaning "fight".
I love the way you can spit these words out.
I'm glad I come from Katoomba
not "Kensington Gardens" or "Pacific Vista".
Maybe we can also change the names of our States?
For Victoria (named after some dead Queen)
give me Pullabooka

for Tasmania — Murrumba
South Australia — Kameruka
New South Wales — Cudgewa
for Queensland — Bulla Bulla
and for Western Australia how about
"People who play stupid football!"
no, OK, how about Wanbi,
meaning "wild dogs" —
I think that says it all.

The new teacher

He must teach Science
    see how he squints
    and looks at his lunch
    like a failed experiment.
Or Maths!
    the grey of his shorts
    the expanse of his ears
    the lovely floral tie & check shirt
    all add up.
He couldn't teach English
    because he's always reading
    and he seems able to string a few words together
    and, as yet,
    he hasn't misspelt his own name.
He's too old to teach History
    and the neat way he packs his briefcase
    implies a sense of place —
    maybe Geography?

No. Well, definitely not Physical Education
        because he doesn't have a moustache
        and he hasn't called anyone "mate" yet
so by class consensus
        we all agree on Industrial Arts
        the fine style of his wig
        gives it away —
that, and his spotless four-wheel drive
        with the "Eat beef, you bastards" sticker
we're sure he'll fit into this school
        like a burger into a bun.

*S*hiver

Sometimes in winter
when the mist buries our suburb
Desiree and I
walk to the golf course
(scene of Dad's weekend despair)
we crawl through the fence
and wander the fairways
    gleaming wet and dark
    in the chill evening.
We sit on the roof of the halfway hut.
I tell Desiree about my poems
    or school
    and try not to mention boys
    or else I'll set Des off!
Desiree talks about her work
    Dad, her clothes
    our house.
But tonight
with the mist closing down
    and dripping heavy from trees
Des tells me of talking to Mum
    just before she died
she tells me of
    the calm woman who held her hand
    and how her eyes never seemed to blink
    as she told Des

that we were the painkillers of her night
and she refused all regrets
in the time she had left
        to brush Desiree's hair back
and tell her what she felt
        the day the doctor diagnosed
and that day was the middle of a heatwave
        but she shivered
as she stepped from the surgery
and saw Dad waiting in the car
and both of us
        waving from the back seat.
But as we drove home
        Des and I told her of our school day
and she knew
        the doctor, the heatwave
        or this death
couldn't touch her
        not with Dad beside her
        and us in the back, talking.

I can feel Des crying beside me
I put my arm around her
we shiver together
        in the mist
and wait for it
            to clear.

The Wild Orchard

Valentine's day

Dear Annabel,

HAPPY VALENTINE'S DAY!
I wanted to give you this card in person,
but my sister told me that Valentine's Day wishes
must remain anomn, anunom, anonomus, nameless.
So, whoever you think I am is probably wrong.
But it's definitely not
Peter Blake, the school captain.
Let's face it, he couldn't even spell his own name,
let alone anonymous!
And it's not Alex Ricco, who seems to act louder
every time you walk past the gang at lunchtime.
Alex is busy right now writing a Valentine
to his basketball.
Anyway, think of nose hair!

Happy Valentine's
J   XXX

Annabel on Jack

He sent me a Valentine's card
    it took him six months to get this far
he almost signed it
he's as transparent as gladwrap
    but I like his smile
and the way he tries to meet my eyes
    and he doesn't play football
so he can't be too bad
    and unlike the rest of the school
he's not in love with baggy pants
    and baseball caps slapped on backwards
he doesn't say "Yo"
or call everyone "brother"
and act like he's from South-Central L.A.
I've never seen him in the company
    of a basketball
    or another girl
so if he gets the courage
    to ask me out
I'll say yes
    and worry about it
later.

I kiss Annabel's photo

I kiss Annabel's photo every night

it's an old voodoo trick
the ghost taught me

for years after Mum died
    I kissed her photo
other kids had teddy bears
    and tapes of Playschool
I cuddled a photo
I tucked myself in with a ghost
    and dreamed
    of holidays that lasted all summer
and parents holding hands
    and games where I always won
and the ghost walked to my room
    to push my hair back
    and smile love.

When Mum wasn't there
    and the holidays dried up
I ripped the photo from the album
and kissed it once every night
    until the ghost came.

So I kiss Annabel's photo
    and work my spell
just long enough to hope.

It can't do any harm
even if it won't do any good
    but you tell that
to the ghost and me.

There's more to life than Annabel

There's more to life than Annabel.
There's Science with Mr Edwards
    rattling his bones as he
    pours one chemical into another
    and on Monday morning
    twenty-eight students concentrate hard
    and hope for an explosion.
There's cold roast-beef sandwiches
    on white bread
    the canteen special on Monday
    and served till Friday.
There's lunchtime
    Ezra and me sitting on the fence
    hoping no-one asks us to join
    in basketball
    or football
    or putting long cold scratches in the duco
    of the Principal's new Volvo.
There's the books from the library
    and the last five I've read
    have been about aliens
    invading the world
    and two teenage heroes with computers
    and I swear I'm ripping up my library card.

There's more to life than Annabel
　　　but not this week
　　　when I've sent her a Valentine
　　　and right now
　　　I'm leaving Ezra on the fence
　　　as I see her walking across the oval
　　　and I'm asking her
　　　out
and was that a smile that creased her mouth …

First date

We're in the back seat
Annabel and me
    our knees are touching
    our elbows
    our legs
    our shoulders
I'm looking straight
    but I can see her
next to me on the bus
    our first date
witnessed by the early evening commuters
of the 482 Express to town.

The next three hours
    Annabel and I
will spend touching
    on the bus
    at the movies
    on the way home
I hope I can stay sane
    all night
not to say anything
    but say enough
not to do anything
    but do enough.

Desiree said
    "just be yourself"
Dad said
    "try to act better than you normally do"
while the ghost smiled all afternoon
    and beckoned me to reflect in the mirror.

I'd like to tell Annabel
    about the ghost
and Desiree's moustache
    and my poetry
but such secrets
    stay hidden
longer than a night on the bus.

Annabel turns and asks what I'm thinking
My Dad whispers
    "I'm thinking about the movie"
Desiree shouts
    "about you Annabel"
the ghost:
    "how nice it is to sit beside you"
as I gulp and ask
    "what do you think of facial hair on women?"
as the bus
    brakes sharply
  at the red light.

Annabel writes poetry

After the movie
    which I can't remember
over coffee tasting of mud
    with the banging of pinball machines
our hands 110 centimetres apart
    on the shiny formica table
one hour left
    to walk home
one hour
    for me to say something
I blurt out the only word I shouldn't:
    "poetry"

and Annabel's eyes,
    dulled by cafe noise and smoke,
flash!
    She writes poetry!
but not about her family
            her friends
            her future
she writes about bodies
            their shape
            the way they walk
the hinge of an arm around a waist
the machine rhythm of gymnastics
the bumping uglies that make brothers & sisters

and I forgot what we said
but we said enough

and I talked about the ghost
    without feeling foolish
and all the way home along Narrowneck Road
    the stars did their stuff
for Annabel and me
    and poetry!

Annabel

Look at her nose
            yes
look at her hair
            yes
at her vegetarian eyes
            yes yes yes

she is a cyclone
a calm
I float I spin
when I touch her arm.

Annabel and the ghost

I'm not scared
　　or embarrassed
I'm excited
　　he's telling me about the ghost
and I can see who she is
　　and it makes perfect sense.
I remember being ten years old
and the stories my Mum
told me late at night
with the Southern Cross
tracking across my bedroom
and Mum making it part of each story
as she sat on the bed.
And Dad's snoring
with Mum whispering "Quiet, George,
you'll wake Annabel"
and how I tried hard not to giggle.
And the pancakes stacked
with strawberries and maple syrup
we'd have every Saturday breakfast
in fact, still have every Saturday
and for seven years I've reached
for a second helping
and winked at Mum.

And as Jack and I walk down Narrowneck Road
I look up at the Southern Cross
and think of Mum and Dad
sleeping now, Dad still snoring
and I think of Jack
at ten years old
alone
hugging a photo
and the ghost
makes complete and perfect sense.

The ghost is away

The ghost didn't come home last night
I waited until dawn
excited
with the news of Annabel and me
I crept into Dad's room
and saw the empty mirror
the clothes in Desiree's room
remained unfolded
Desiree asleep in her Levi's
and the echo of the ghost
hung loose
I climbed out the window
and sat on the roof
one eye on the chimney
thinking of a ghost parading as Santa
the Southern Cross faded
as the sun crept up the mountain
and I called the ghost
and called again
and felt nine years old
waiting for Mum to come home
so I could tell her my day before I slept.

I climbed back through the window and into bed
and thought of Annabel
but she had the face of the ghost
and I must have dozed
as I woke sweating.
I looked at the calendar
seven years today
my Mum died
and now I know
why the ghost
is away.

The fireplace

Our house has a fireplace
one of those slow-combustion models
with the glass door
and the soot-black internal chimney.
My Dad cuts the Ironbark
with an axe he's had since he was a kid
the sound of chopping
is the winter pulse of this suburb.
At night, Desiree moves her chair
close to the fire
and talks on the phone
Dad rests his coffee on the grill
to keep it warm
while he goes out into the mist
for another log.
At midnight, alone, I open the fireplace door
and feed my poems on Annabel
to the flame.
The words dance with a heat and light
they never had on the page
each flicker warming my hands.
I go back to my room
to write some more food
for the fire burning
in this house.

*E*zra finds the hut

If you follow the bush track
    off Narrowneck Road for 500 metres
you'll see the ghost gum
    the one with the arrow
    pointing west
follow that track
    until you reach the bridge
before the creek
    there's an overgrown wallaby track
push through it
    until you see the tree
    with Jack & Annabel's initials.
Quiet now.
    look up at the ridge
    on the left
see the hut
    built by bushwalkers fifty years ago
if you go there after school
    you'll find Annabel & Jack
but hey,
    don't go there after school.

*M*egalong creek hut

Ever since Desiree told me about this hut
I knew it would be the special place
        for Annabel and me
somewhere silent.
        her parents
my Dad
        even the ghost couldn't find us here.
we've cleaned it
        evicted the resident possum
nailed the walls and roof back
        the wind still creeps in
but we hold each other to keep warm
we take turns to tell stories
as the trees brush against the roof
and the world clouds over
        in the winter afternoon.
We've planned a night alone here
        but
neither of us has that much courage
one ghost is enough to handle.
        still
every afternoon with the thought of homework
and school fading
we run through the bush
to our special place
        and disappear
                from sight.

Annabel and the wild orchard

Sometimes I don't want to reach our hut
I want to take Jack's hand
follow the trail
        down to the six foot track
pick up a snake stick
        and like an old miner
follow that track to the valley
and there, with Jack,
        set up camp
pick apples from the wild orchard
        watch Jack try to build a fire
and when he's sweating with frustration
        offer him the matches
and laugh all through dinner
        and at night watch the stars
no higher than the cliff walls
and the two of us
holding tight for warmth
as sleep wraps around
        we dream in the soil
        of our days
        moist, firm, full
until the sun
        wakes
and offers us time
        to walk
        holding hands
in the wild orchard.

Making a Living

The funeral

We were twelve
the dead bird on the steps
Ezra touched the matted feathers
    with a stick
and wondered aloud
why it flew into a closed window.
We got Dad's shovel
buried it under the fir tree
lashed two sticks together
wrote RIP on the cross-stick
and stood looking at the grave
Ezra said he'd never seen
    anything dead before
I said I had
    and walked back to the house.

*D*esiree

Late at night
    when Jack and Dad are asleep
I stand naked in my bedroom
    in front of the mirror
I look at my breasts
    in the surgery fluorescent light
of my Mother's death
    I touch them
feel my nipples harden unwillingly
    it can kill me
this thing, this woman thing.
    I find a different lump every night
and lie awake
    wishing it away.
My last boyfriend tried to understand
    he even offered to inspect them for me
his hand made me forget, for a time
    but I know
it's not the cancer
    or the pain
it's the waiting
    as I pull the sweater
gently
    over my head.

*C**areers*

It's Careers Advice Week
where a very serious man
    in a white shirt and thin black tie
talks to us, individually, about our futures.
With ten per cent unemployment
and all of us desperate to avoid
    thinking about next year
I don't like his chances.
When Ezra saw him yesterday
    he told the Advisor that his ambition
    was to never see his father again.
Now, knowing Ezra's father
    this seemed a worthy occupation
the Advisor handed Ezra a TAFE Handbook
    and made another appointment.
I've decided with my five minutes
    I'm going to talk non-stop
    and, hopefully, walk out.

I'm going to tell him
    I want to marry Annabel
    write a book of poems
        even people like him could read
    buy a house on a cliff
    find a cure for nose hair
    win a medal at the Poetry Olympics*
    be interviewed regularly on television
and never enter a school again
and never wear a white shirt with a thin black tie.

* POETRY OLYMPICS actually happen. The idea
was originated in London by poet Michael Horowitz

Selling up

Last night
a Real Estate Agent visited.
Dad showed him the house
        the view
    avoided the cubbyhouse
    promised to trim the hedge
they sat down and talked money
    and buyers moving west
    Interest Rates
    the chance of a quick sale
and all through the meeting
    Dad kept looking around
    as though somebody was watching him
until the Agent got worried
    left his card
    told Dad to "discuss it with the wife"

by then
    Desiree and I knew
we weren't selling
    because Mum
had already made her views
    hauntingly clear.

The wreck

last night
I dreamed I died.
A car accident
Ezra beside me
in the wreck
his teeth dripping with blood
we hung upside down
one breath away from the cliff edge
with the ghost gum holding our sway
and I touched Ezra
and shivered
I struggled to the door
and pushed
as the tree surrendered
we toppled
the car, Ezra, me
kept falling
until I landed
this morning.

Dad didn't come home last night

Dad didn't come home last night
me and the ghost waited
listened for the tyre crunch on the drive
for the drunken key in the lock
the ghost wasn't worried
she sat in front of her mirror
and looked at the family photos.
I lay in bed
    thinking of road accidents
    back street gangs
    police RBT units on the highway
then I remembered the woman
the one Dad refused to tell us about
    as he nervously straightened his tie
    and combed his hair (first time this week).

I thought I was the one
        supposed to be out all Saturday night
        not my fifty-year-old father!
why am I alone in bed
        with my sensible pyjamas
        and a good book?
why is Desiree snoring
        when our father's out on the town
        and we're home by midnight

and why, why is the ghost still smiling
        does she know something I don't …

Sunday lunch

Cold chicken, fresh bread
Dad and me on the veranda
Dad still in last night's clothes
we eat quietly
as he tells me
about his only big date in seven years.
The dinner, the wine
their children in every glass
and all the time
Dad's trying to flirt
until dessert
when he gives up and tells
this woman of his wife and her death
and the years drinking early evening
with his workmates
and coming home to us
and the photos on his dresser
and over coffee it takes hours
to tell a life story
and to listen to hers
and that's what they did all night
(a rueful smile over our chicken).
He talked all night, and listened.

he didn't mention his work
he talked like he's talking to me now
he talked until he knew
        the ghost still haunted him
        and always would.

This morning Dad came home
        to the photos on the dresser
and planned another big date
        seven years from today.

The earthquake

The earth moved last night
the ancient plates under our mountain shifted
    as windows spooked and rattled
    the lampshade cracked
and our wedding photo
    fell off the dresser.
Desiree slept
Jack snored
    I fastened the window
    turned off the lamp
    picked up the photo
and spent an hour holding the frame
    getting married all over again
while the earth
    threatened.

This morning
    the papers reported
    3.5 on the Richter Scale
    and no damage
I didn't mention the wedding
    but all morning I felt
    the cruel aftershock.

What I do for a living

I spend my day in front of this ignorant computer
typing stories
no, not stories (stories have heart)
typing articles
on our trade deficit and unemployment figures
so people can read and worry over their cornflakes.
At lunch I cross Broadway
for a drink and a sandwich
forgetting my health deficit and waistline figures.
The other night Desiree asked me
why I wanted to be a journalist
and it took me exactly forty-nine minutes to
    think of an answer
and that was a simple "for the money"
because during forty-eight of those forty-nine
minutes
I remembered their childhood
    Jack's first day at school
    his little wave
    as the teacher lead him away
    and Desiree's laugh every morning
    at something on television
    and how it woke the house

and I realised I don't give a stuff
about politics, or inflation,
or rising interest rates,
as long as I keep hearing Desiree's laugh
and seeing Jack's pride
then I know what I really do
        for a living.

All her brain cells

I know why Desiree
        doesn't have a boyfriend
        and hasn't had one
        for a long time.
it's because
        she has perfect eyesight
        and all her brain cells.

Solo Desiree

Jack and Annabel have made love
I can tell
Jack doesn't bother me any more with questions
    on girls, or sex,
      or what he should do about his appearance.
He looks like one of those TV evangelists
    who've discovered God
    and the miracle of money
it's almost unbearable, his swagger,
    but at least
he doesn't brag out loud.
Annabel's OK too!
I spent the first hour after meeting her
    looking at her top lip
and I'm pleased to report
    there's a good trace of darkening hair
and thank Christ she doesn't giggle!
    or talk about music.

Even Dad liked her
        but I think he was just happy to see Jack
        bring a friend home
although he doesn't seem so pleased
when he meets my boyfriends
not that there's been anyone for a while
I'm going through my Nun stage
you know, wearing black
                talking quietly
                keeping my desires religiously confined
but not for much longer.
        If Jack and Annabel keep pawing each other
        when I'm watching television
I'm breaking my vows
        problem is,
men are easy to get rid of
        harder to find.

The ghost spoke to me last night

The ghost spoke to me last night
I was sleeping
I turned to the window where she sat
she whispered for me to tell Desiree
to stop looking into the mirror
and then she disappeared

the next morning
I told Desiree
she didn't believe me at first
then she gave me a kiss
went to her room
and came out in her favourite dress
and white stockings
she said she was having the day off
Dad smiled, and said he was too
they both looked at me, pleading
for me to jig school

this house is going mad.

*F*ather of the year

It's been a month since Dad had his big date
in that time he's devoted
every Saturday to Des and me
we've been out for lunch
              to the movies
              on a ferry cruise
and last week we camped the night
       in the Blue Gum Forest
Des and I are worried we'll never get rid of him!
He talks to me about Annabel
       and encourages Desiree to go out more
he tries to cook dinner
we have long involved talks
       on our life, our school, our future
it's like living with your Deputy Principal.

I've seen Dad in my room
    looking at my wall photos
he's started ironing Desiree's clothes
twice he's increased our allowance
he's talking of us going on holiday together
he said I could bring Annabel
and Desiree could bring anyone
    (Desiree looked ill)
he's stopped drinking wine with dinner
he cuts the fat off his meat
last week I saw him preparing to go jogging
I occasionally catch him looking at me as I read
    he looks satisfied
he gets home early from work
    and wants to play cricket with me in the backyard
he sits alone in the cubbyhouse
    staring across the valley
he says "nigh nigh" to us, as though we're
      children again.
Our Dad is going for father of the year
and slowly sending Desiree and me
completely mad.

Annabel writes a poem for english

I have been told by my English teacher
    she with the nervous twitch
    and perfect vowels
    stolen from British movies at the Savoy
that I should write a poem
    as an assignment
    and that the poem should be on NATURE,
    and I should make full use of
simile, metaphor, and alliteration.

Now, I like birds, and streams,
    and the odd tree as much as anyone
    but if I'm told to do something
    so bloody narrow again I'll
I'll
I'll

Nature
  (A poem with simile, metaphor, & alliteration)
the King Parrot
    drops like a stone
        like my Dad when he's drunk
        like a Nun's eyes before God

the King Parrot
      is stone
      is drunk
      is dead
dead door-nail dead darkly
definitely damn dead (oh dear!)

And as I hand this limp piece of protest
to my teacher
I see my English marks drop faster than
faster than
faster than a dead parrot!

Winter Annabel

I'm sick of people talking about
    this country as being only
    sun, beaches, and the outback.
Where I live it's cold, windy,
and the mist drops heavy in January.
While people fry on Bondi
I wear an overcoat and a wet nose
    and every house
    keeps a stack of firewood ready all summer.
Sure, it only snows a few times a year
but those winds punching through Megalong Valley
    make my teeth ache with cold
and I love it all!

I've never seen the sense
    in lying comatose on a pile of sand
    turning pink
    or swimming in each other's effluent
    that passes as surf.
And I like how the rail-thin *Dolly* victims
    in Year 11 desperately try to look slim
    in two jumpers and an overcoat.
My idea of fashion is a flannelette shirt
    and Levis in front of the fireplace.

People say the beach is the great equaliser
who are they kidding?
sit at Bondi and watch the boys flex
        and the girls walk bolt upright
        it looks like a nightmare episode of *Baywatch*.
The true equaliser is the mountain cold
        and stacks of clothes flung together
maybe then we'd listen to what each other is saying
        instead of checking out the best bods.

And as I wrap another layer
        around my Size 10
I think of Jack's favourite saying:
"today's tan is tomorrow's cancer".

I walk outside
and whistle at the wind.

Echoes

My son is seeing a girl

My son is seeing a girl
    and a ghost.
I hear him talking to Annabel
    in the chill afternoon
and I hear whispers
    to the ghost
in the long night.
I haven't told him I know.
What could I say?
In the past year
    he has grown tall
    his eyes sparkle the way of his mother's
and when he's reading
    I look at him with pride.

I know who the ghost is
I'm glad they talk
    I stare into the mirror
as the trees shadow through the window
    and I envy Jack.

I lean against the wall and listen.

He is talking to her
    a soft monologue
    that pumps through this house
    like an open vein.

I try to picture the ghost
    sitting at the edge of his bed
and the night grows suddenly dark
    and the whispers fade.

I return to bed
and wrap the blankets of memory
around me, tight.

Sex, sport, and nose hair (according to Annabel)

Sex is what Jack and I practise at Megalong Creek.
Sex is my parents encouraging me to go out
    early Saturday night, so they can "talk".
Sex leers over my shoulder at the canteen.
Sex is the colour of the December bushfires
    with our hut feeling their hot breath.
Sex is what the school terms "personal development"
    as our parents look worried.

Sport is my Dad's idea of a Sunday out.
Sport is a short skirt in winter
    tossing a netball through the mist
    while our teacher sips coffee.
Sport does something to the brain of an everyday
male.
Sport rumbles down the stairs
    knocking Year 7s over
    as it swings its gorilla arms to the oval.

Nose Hair is what Jack thinks of more than me
Nose Hair tickles as we kiss
Nose Hair grows and grows and grows
Nose Hair is the forward brother of ear hair
Nose Hair longs to be plucked!

Blue mountains school

The clouds cover our school
as impenetrable as Science
        on a Friday afternoon
the black cockatoos crunch nuts
        and drop them from trees
like bombs cracking the schoolyard

Annabel and me on the seat
        our lips feeling their way
through the mist
when the Deputy Principal Mrs Jonestown
        like a tank
        comes lumbering through the murk
        guns blazing
        horn-rimmed glasses
        like heat-seeking missiles
aimed at Annabel and me

and she starts on with that
        "what sort of example is this to the
             Juniors" stuff
and I try to defend with
        "no one can see us in this cloud"
but with the predictability of someone over thirty
        she shoots a "does that make it all right"

and now would not be the time
to mention love, peace,
and an end to the Cold War I fear
so we're marched back to class
prisoners of war
sentenced
to six months hard labour
and 2-Unit Maths
and the clouds come in thicker
soft cages
          hiding tanks clanking
around the perimeter fence
waiting …

Bloody rain

"Bloody rain" says Mr Chivers
bouncing a basketball
on the one dry patch of court
"bloody rain" he nods to our Sports class
and gives us the afternoon off.
Bloody rain all right
as Annabel and I run to Megalong Creek hut
faster than we ever have in Chivers's class
and the exercise we have in mind
we've been training for all year
but I doubt if old Chivers
will give us a medal if he ever finds out.
We high-jump into the hut
and strip down
climb under the blankets
and cheer the bloody rain
as it does a lap or two
around the mountain
while Annabel and me
embrace like winners should
        like good sports do
as Mr Chivers sips his third coffee
and twitches the bad knee
from his playing days

while miles away
Annabel and I
score a convincing victory
and for once in our school life
the words "Physical Education"
make sense ...

Confessions

"I like the back of your neck"

> her fingers roam
> untouched but hopefully washed territory
> I feel a twitch in my knee
> (of all places!)

"I like your ears"

> I've seen my Dad's ears grow big
> and old with him. The elephant
> with his memory in the mirror

"I like your mouth"

> but only when it's shut, or silent,
> keep it silent Jack
> the wet of our kiss soaks my insides

"I like your hair"

> my Dad again
> haircut like a McDonald's arch
> retreating to the safety of bald

"I like your eyes"

I look straight
think only of the Kurdish soldier
facing his firing squad
seeing beyond, and never looking back.

"I like your arms"

Annabel, give in. Just admit it
I'm your kind of guy
I'm perfect, OK.
What can you find to fault

"but about your nose hair, Jack …"

The right reasons

I've been sitting here
trying to think of the one thing in my life
that will give it sense,
like they do in Hollywood movies
and after ninety minutes of formula
you get a happy family
with blonde children
and the wife always looks younger than she should
and the hero looks older
and the credits roll happily ever after
while Annabel and I walk along Narrowneck Road
knowing her parents are away
but I'm still thinking of this one thing
and all I get is

a nine-year-old boy
ducking wild plovers dive-bombing the schoolyard
thinking
    "what if they hit my eye"
or a twelve-year-old
riding beside the train tracks
looking for bits of human left
after the train smash
    "what if I find some skin
    what if I find some skin".

At fourteen, I'm standing in a pack of boys
waiting for the ball
so we can avoid bashing heads
and for once it comes my way
and I dive full-length to meet it
        "what if I meet someone's boot
        what if I meet someone's boot"
but I'm lucky, I score,
and no one has to mention fear for another week
or until now

when Annabel and I are in bed together
and I thought football and death
and blindness and parents and school
and alcohol and unlicensed cars
were scary
and you move one arm under my body
and your skin is not hard like
        the gloss of magazines
or cold like the railroad metal
or brittle like the beak of a dead plover

and I'm thinking as our bodies meet
that I'll remember this forever
and I just hope
it's for all the right reasons.

The bike ride

Annabel has the bottle
I carry maps and food
I'm scared of getting lost
she wants to cycle aimless
she pedals like a caged mouse
she checks her watch
she feels her pulse
she ties the knot of her hair
      tight against her neck
she smiles for me to lead
I strain to follow the curve of her road
I hear the birds chorus
      to witness such clatter
I am leaning over the handlebars
my shoes pull hard on the pedals
I breathe her scent with the headwind
She rests her thigh on the seat
      turns to wait for me
we ride double-file
we hold hands
      swing to keep balance

she tells me stories
I tell jokes
we suck water from the bottle as we ride
we stop
kiss with our mouths full
we blow water into each other's mouth
she smiles
I can feel the crease of her lips
We are in love with this bike ride.

*M*onday, the last before holidays

Monday, the last before holidays
Ezra and I walk to school
his plaster off, the skin still white
he tells me his father is moving out
later I watch him smile all through Maths.
Monday, the last before holidays
I see Annabel walk up to a bunch of guys
heckling this Year 8 girl
and punch the biggest guy
hard, cracking his smile
she walks away with the girl
and the school holds its breath
I write in my diary
never cross Annabel
never cross Annabel.
Monday, the last before holidays
rumour has it that
two Science teachers are to marry
and honeymoon at Surfers
this confirms our suspicions
that teachers like bank tellers
and public servants
in-breed with immunity.

Monday, the last before holidays
the Principal tells a joke during Assembly
and everyone laughs
not because it was funny
or his timing was right
or even that we understood it
but, after all,
it was
Monday, the last before holidays.

*M*s Curling

Ms Curling and I had a talk recently
not about my late essay
or laughing in class
or even my excuse for a uniform
we had a talk about sex
sex and AIDS
sex and babies
sex and Annabel
it was very interesting
watching my favourite teacher
tell me stuff I already knew
and squirm with embarrassment
Ms Curling looks very attractive
when embarrassed
particularly when I asked her about Annabel
how did she know?
was she taught this at University?
was there a subject called
        "STUDENTS HAVING SEX — how to find out"?
did she get top marks?
so we skipped Annabel
and discussed condoms
I said I liked orange ones
        and we ended our talk, in laughter.

Ms Curling and I sat together sometimes after that
I told her about the hut near Megalong Creek
        about my Dad not coming home
        about Desiree
Ms Curling said she'd like to meet my Dad
I said he was too old for her

I didn't know there were teachers like her
I thought the years of exposure to Year 9
dried them out,
made them brittle, hard.
she was OK
maybe I would let her meet my Dad …
I'm sure the ghost would approve.

Annabel kisses

Annabel kisses like the wind whistling
through the wattle
Annabel kisses like a prayer I said
at the age of nine
I couldn't open my eyes for hours
Annabel kisses and our fireplace glows
Annabel kisses and the nuns at St Rita's
turn their heads
Annabel kisses as the dogs bark
Annabel kisses on October 6th
all afternoon
two days before my birthday
Annabel kisses and even the ghost is silent
Annabel kisses with red lipstick
and her hand softly
on my wrist
Annabel kisses and I think of toothpaste
the 1992 Grand Final
and the beach on a family holiday
Annabel kisses with her eyes open
Annabel kisses in her black dress
with silver buttons
Annabel kisses with a sharp intake
of breath
Annabel kisses me
Annabel kisses me
       and I kiss back.

It's easy

It's easy to tell your Mum
you're in love
with the guy from up the road
and that you and him
made love in your bed with the birthday sheets
when they were on holidays last weekend.
It's easy to ask for a second helping of guilt
and misplaced trust
as you share tea
with two spoons of tears
and a dash of broken promises.
It's easy to invite Jack for dinner
with the family
and feel his hand under the table
while you watch your Mum
reach for the carving knife
as Jack asks for a second helping.
It's easy to see the fear
in your Dad's eyes
as he struggles to make sense
of camping trips and story books
and Girl Guide meetings every Thursday
and his pride when I won the high jump
on his forty-fifth birthday
and tonight he looks at Jack
like he looks at his car when it won't start

it's easy
easy as kissing your childhood goodbye.

She is the reason I walk home from school
    the long way
She talks all breath and throat
She keeps my picture on the wall
    next to a STOP sign
She says poetry books make good weapons
She says I look like a movie star
    I say Keanu Reeves
    she says, no, Roger Rabbit.
She listens to Madonna and Opera at the same time
She spoons sugar in her coffee
    but refuses to stir
She wears Egyptian sandals in summer
    I float down her Nile
She knocks at my door and shouts
    "Police. Open Up."

She wears black stockings with red flowers
She wears black stockings with Baxter boots
She wears black stockings
    I follow her step
She eats with a fork
    stays afraid of the knife
She kisses me in front of my Dad
    we all look out the window
She rides a bicycle like a threat
She says Maths teachers were born
    with glasses and bad haircuts
She likes Science
    but refuses to cut up the frog
She clenches her fist
    as we walk past McDonalds
She is waiting
    here
    now
She says love is like a shadow
    that scares you awake
She refuses to say more.

Telling the ghost

I'm going to tell the ghost to stay away
I don't know how I'm going to do it
but
I am going to
how long do you need a ghost for?
how long is Dad going to
    say I look like you
    carry your photo in his wallet
    mention you every night over dinner
I'll be seventeen in two weeks time
Annabel and I are having a private party
    in the hut
and then I'm coming home to Dad and Desiree, and
    dinner.
At midnight, I'm going to tell the ghost
    no more visits
it's not that I don't need her
    or want her to stay
I'm just too old to believe in it any more
seven years of talking to myself
seven years of listening
    and hearing a fading echo
    of a Mother I loved, and still do.

I'll just tell her straight
    blow a kiss
    smile (definitely won't cry)
and get on with this life.
I've decided it's time
I've got more than a memory
I see my Mother
    in my face
    in Desiree's hair, and her hands,
    in what we do in this world.
I know she'll understand
it's time
I definitely won't cry
at least
not until she's gone.

Echoes

I woke early, dressed
climbed out the window
and sat on our roof
to watch the morning
I could hear the gang-gangs
welcoming the day
I knew I had a full hour
to sit here, and wait.
For the first time in my life
I'm waiting for NOTHING to happen.
I'm seventeen
I've cut my nose hair
    dressed in clothes my sister would approve of
I've washed the childhood from my eyes
I'm sitting on this roof
and I'm happy because all I can see
    are trees, the rising mist,
    the orange cliffs
    and our cubbyhouse, still standing.
I know in one hour my Dad will wake
    and cast his eyes to her photo
    and he'll know what his day lacks
    before he's had a chance to change it.

He needs his ghost
    whispering through the house
    arranging the days into sequence.
I climb down from the roof
    and walk around our yard.
I am alone
the only ghost I hear is the wind
I walk along Narrowneck Road
    past Annabel's house
    down to the Landslide Cliff
and for the last time
I shout the ghost's name
and turn
    without waiting for the echo.

A Place Like This

Dedicated to Leonie Tyle, Robyn Sheahan,
and Glen Leitch for their support and belief

CONTENTS

go

this quiet land

screwed

a place like this

weird

a young orchard

Go

*J*ack

I'm not unemployed.
I'm just not working at the moment.
School now seems a distant shame
    of ball games, half-lies at lunch time,
    and teachers fearing the worst.
I'm not studying either.
Yeah, I got into Uni,
    so did Annabel.
Two Arts degrees does not a life make.
So we both chucked it.
University is too serious.
I'm eighteen years old,
    too young to work forever
    too old to stay home.
Annabel and I make love most afternoons,
    which, as you can imagine,
    passes the time
    but
I don't think we can make money out of it,
or learn much, although, we have learnt something ...

I want to leave town
I want to leave town
I want to leave.

Jack's Dad

What can I tell you about my Dad?
Years ago I would have said
an ill-fitting suit, brown shoes,
a haircut of nightmares,
and a job, in the city.
That's all.
That's what I would have said.
And a dead wife.
Long dead. Dead yesterday.
No difference.

But not now.
Now, he tries.
He reads the paper with courage.
He never shakes his head when I'm late home.
He's forty-two years of hope
        eight years of grief, and
        two years of struggle.

Let me tell you this one thing about my father,
and leave it at that.

Friday night, two months ago.
I'm trying to sleep,
when I hear this soft bounce, every few seconds,
and the backyard floodlight is on.

It's midnight,
and there's a man in the yard.
I grab the cricket bat from the hall cupboard,
check my sister's room, she's asleep,
still in her Levi's and black top
(I like that top — I gave it to her
for her birthday, and she always wears it.
Sorry, I better go bash this burglar …)

Where's my father when the house needs defending?
At the pub? At work?
Not at midnight surely?
I grip the bat,
wish I'd taken cricket more seriously at school.
I open the door slightly,
think of newspaper headlines —
"HERO DIES SAVING HOUSE"
"CRIME WAVE SOARS OUT WEST"
"HIT FOR SIX!"

There's that bounce again,
and the figure bends to pick something up
(a gun! a knife!)

A cricket ball!
What!

He runs and bowls a
slow drifting leg-spinner, hits middle stump.
Dad turns,
whispers "howzat!"
and walks to pick up the ball again.

What can I do?
My Dad, midnight cricket,
and a well-flighted leg-spinner.

I walk out to face up
tapping the bat gently.
Dad smiles and bowls a wrong-un.
The bastard knocks my off-stump out.
He offers me a handshake and advice.
"Bat and pad together son,
  don't leave the gate open.
  Let's have one more over shall we?"

He goes back to his mark,
polishing the ball on his pyjamas,
every nerve twitching,
every breath involved.

The stumbling bagpipes

We make love every Tuesday afternoon.
I kiss her eyelids
and rub my hand along her arm
to feel the soft hair
that shines in the fading light.
Sometimes the clouds float
up the valley
and the rain dances on our window
as the parrots fly for home.
I kiss her shoulders and her neck
and we try breathing slowly, in time,
under the doona.

There's a young boy next door
who's practicing the bagpipes.
He stands on the veranda
and scares hell out of the dogs.
They howl in time
as he blows himself hoarse.

We love that sound,
discordant, clumsy, feverish.
It reminds us of that first Tuesday afternoon,
two years ago,

trying to make love before
Annabel's parents got home.
We agreed on further practice.

That's why we celebrate like this,
every Tuesday,
me and Annabel,
and the stumbling bagpipes.

What Dad said

This is what Dad said
when I told him about me and Annabel
wanting to drive and not come back
for a year or so …

"Son." (When he says *son* I know a story
      is not far behind.)
"Son. When I was eighteen
I'd already decided to ask your Mum to marry me.
And I had my journalism degree half-finished.
I wanted my own desk, my own typewriter,
a home to put them in, and I wanted your Mum.
She said yes, and the rest followed.
At twenty-two, we had this home.
At twenty-two, I learned gardening.
You know the big golden ash in the corner?
I planted that first year here.
Most of our friends were going overseas,
taking winter holiday work in the snow,
or getting drunk every night at the pub.
At twenty-two, your Mum and I
were sitting on the veranda with a cup of cocoa
and a fruit cake.
I'm fifty-two years old this August.
You're a smart kid Jack. A smart kid.

I think you and Annabel should get out of here
as fast as possible. Have a year doing anything
you want. My going-away present is enough money
to buy a car, a cheap old one OK. You'll have to
work somewhere to buy the petrol, and to keep going.
But go."

Let me tell you
it wasn't what I expected.

But maybe, just maybe,
I understand the old man more now.
More than I ever have.

*F*or once in my life

When Jack told me last night
about leaving
what I really wanted to say
was *NO*.
Like a father should.
NO.
And I had all the words ready,
all the clichés loaded
but I couldn't do it.
He looked so hungry,
so much in need of going
that I gave him my first big speech in years,
only this time it was one he wanted to hear.
So that's it.

When Jack was asleep last night
I went into his room.
I sat beside his bed
        and listened to his breathing.
I don't know for how long.
I listened,
and with each breath
I felt his yearning, and confidence,
and strength.
I walked out of his room
sure I'd said the right thing

maybe not as a father
but as a Dad.
I'd said the right thing,
for once in my life.

A *1974 Corona*

It's a 1974 Corona sedan
that's been driven by a
middle-aged single bank manager
called Wilbur who never went out on the weekend
except for a Sunday morning drive with his Mum
to church five kilometres down the road
and enjoyed cleaning it's dull brown duco
every Saturday instead of
    watching the football
    getting drunk
    doing overtime
    or playing with snappy children.

All I had to do was give him $1200
and a handshake to drive it home,
through a mudpuddle or two,
and take that crucifix off the mirror,
give it to the kid next door,
and maybe even consider a paint job …

but no, let's leave it brown.
Bank manager brown.
That's my car.
That's my ticket with Annabel, out of here.

Annabel on Jack

Jack reads too many books.
He thinks we're going to drive all year
and have great adventures.
He thinks the little money
we have will last.
He wants to sleep in the car,
cook dinner over an open fire.
I'm just waiting for him to
pack a fishing line, smiling,
saying "we can live off the land".
Jesus Christ.
I'm not gutting a fish and cooking it.
But
I do want to go,
even if it only lasts a month or two.
Even if we drive to Melbourne and back
and don't talk to another person.
I want to go.
Why?
Because I've never
been more than 200 kilometres from home,
and that was with my parents, on holiday.
And because Jack's smart,
but not that smart, if you know what I mean.
You watch.
First week, we'll be out of money,

sleeping near a smelly river,
eating cold baked beans out of a can.
The car will have a flat battery
and Jack will be saying something like,
"Isn't this great. Back to nature.
Living off the land. Not a care in the world."
Jesus Christ.

Jack driving

I love to drive,
to blast back to boyhood
where I dreamt of a highway,
a car with a floor-shift
and nowhere to sleep for a week,
burning rubber and a dare
to take every bend
faster than advised.
Even now
I think of a blow-out
as a test for how steady
my hands are on the wheel,
my knuckles white with impatience.
Me, Annabel and
the stereo sing,
trucks threaten our dreams
like thunder,
as we reach the hill
curse the oncoming lights,
I strain to keep the revs up
as we crest the rise,
I snap into top
glide down the mountain
escape ramp 500 metres ahead,
we don't need it.

Two days out

Two days out.
Last night we slept in the car.
Yes, by a river, as I predicted.
Not smelly though.
Clean. Surprisingly clean.
Jack and I had a bath in it.
A naked goose pimple bath.
We raced each other from bank to bank.
We even used soap.
My Mum's going-away present.
Soap-on-a-rope. It floats!

We lay on the grass.
The sun dried our white bodies.
We did nothing for as long as possible.

In the quiet afternoon
we drove for hours.
Jack said, "I'm hungry"
and the bloody car slowed to a stop.
Jack looking at me,
me at Jack,
and neither of us knowing why.
Then I looked at the petrol gauge.
Empty.

Empty, and food, cold river baths
and the nearest town
were all a million miles away.
Two days out …

As I stood on the lonely backroad,
I'm sure I heard birds,
kookaburras,
laughing …

The ride

"You two heading anywhere special?"
he says, changing down gear, double-clutching
and churning the old truck's insides loud.
Annabel and I look at each other.
What's this mean?
I decide to answer a question with a question.
I learnt that in Year 9
and it hasn't failed me yet.
"Why?"

"Why. Because I got fifty acres of ripe apples
and a town full of unemployed kids that
hate the sight of them, that's why.
And my kids and I can't pick fifty acres
in two years, much less two months.
I'll pay you, give you a place to sleep.
That's if you're interested?"

The truck cabin rattles over potholes.
He winds down the window
and flicks his cigarette out.

It's not what I'm expecting.
Two days away, out of petrol, and offered a job.
I wanted to get as far as possible,
not a few hundred kilometres down the road.

But it's money. And a place to stay.
Annabel squeezes my hand and I know
it's a *yes* squeeze.
I squeeze back and before I can answer
Annabel says,
'Sure mister. We'll take it. I like apples."

George smiles and says,
"You'll be picking Miss, not eating them."

But he's all right.
Anyone who drives a truck this old can't be too bad.

This Quiet Land

Haybales

It was from a book I read in school.
Two teenagers and a shed full
    of stacked haybales,
a crow's nest in the loft,
and her father, the farmer, in town.
I can't remember anything else but
these two, barely fifteen years old,
lying up high on the bales
and the boy with his hand
    up her dress,
and they're both shaking,
even though it's summer outside.
She takes off her dress,
her bra, and undies,
stands on the highest bale
and gestures him up.
And in a tumble of straw and clothes
they made nervous love
page after page.
First from his side,
    all awkward, lopsided, and flush.
Then hers,
    sweat and itch and eyes on the crow's nest.
I kept that book for years.
And when George offered us his shed to sleep in,
I said *yes*,
and asked if it had haybales …

The farm

The road goes through a path of pines.
It's dusty and hot, but here, for a while,
the trees hold the cool and dark,
then a sharp left and you see the wooden house,
surrounded by wattles and a sagging fence.
Two kids run out,
no more than ten years old,
both jump on the tray while the truck's still moving,
country kids.
There's someone else, older,
sixteen maybe, a girl,
standing in the dirt of the drive,
wearing overalls and dusty riding boots,
and when we turn to park near the shed,
I see she's pregnant.
George says, "that's Emma, my eldest",
as the four dogs start barking all at once,
sniffing our hands and boots,
and running around George, jumping up,
and not stopping barking,
not for a second.

*C*raig

I'm Craig. I'm ten next week.
You come to pick apples for us?
You gunna stay? Lots don't stay,
reckon it's too hard.
Reckon Dad don't pay enough.
Reckon we're stupid to live this far from town.
You gunna stay?
We need help, Dad says.
Now Emma can't pick.
She's pregnant you know.
Gunna have twins, or three, or four.
She's so big. Bigger than a cow.
Bigger than a house.
She couldn't climb the ladder to pick now.
You ever picked before?
I can pick two bins a day.
I reckon it's good for football training.
You two married?
You're not gunna get pregnant are you?
Anyway, I'll see ya.
My sister's name is Beck, she's seven.
She don't talk much.
Not like me.
See ya.

*T*his quiet land

It's nothing more than an irrigation channel
dug across the plains,
but George, despite his eye on the harvest
    and it's price,
years before built a hardwood landing
to dive off into the cool water.
Annabel and I spend every afternoon
    after picking
lying on the wet timber
    listening to the frogs
and watching the dragonflies skim across the surface.

What can I say?
When we know George is in town
    or too busy hosing down the tractor
we strip naked and worship the late breeze
blowing ripples across the channel.
A beer or two and I'm set for life.
A beer or two and Annabel's lips
    and her arm resting on my stomach
    and I hope to never leave
the late afternoon
    of tired muscles, channel water,
    and this quiet land.

*T*he shed

Me and Annabel are sitting against the shed.
In the sun.
Sunday. No work.
I'm dreaming of a month of Sundays.
We've been working for two weeks.
Our hands are starting to heal
　　from the first week of learning
　　to snap the stem of each apple
　　as we plucked it.
　　Yes, "pluck", that's what George says.
George loves his apples so much
　　he can't bear to just pick them.
　　He plucks them quick, yet soft,
　　places them in his bag
　　and when it's full
　　leans over the bin and releases the latch.
He fills four, sometimes five bins a day.
That first week Annabel and I averaged three together,
from 7am to 5pm. Climbing ladders with the bag
half-full,
swinging in front, pulling your neck forward.
I cursed my luck for running out of petrol.

The second week was easier.
George gave us the heavy trees, loaded down,
until the weight broke the branches.

We filled four bins a day. By Friday, it was five.
Twenty Dollars a bin.
George says we're all right.
So "alright" last night he came into the shed
with a dozen bottles of beer.

I like the sun when I'm tired.
I lay down,
close my eyes and think of
anything but apples.

Craig on his Mum

Mum ran away from us
the night Beck vomited all over the dinner.
She didn't take much,
except the blind cat and all our money.
Well, that's what Dad said.
Beck vomited all over everyone's dinner.
It was unreal. I don't know if that's why Mum left,
but she left,
and for weeks I kept thinking she was hiding
somewhere on the farm,
in the shed,
or camping down by the channel,
and I kept hoping she'd just
come walking back into the kitchen,
but that hasn't happened.

I'm learning to cook now.
So is Beck.
We get our own breakfast and lunch,
and sometimes we cook dinner —
you know, spaghetti and some sauce,
from a jar.
Emma can cook, pretty good too.
I miss Mum sometimes,
and I know Beck does too,
but Beck hasn't vomited since.

Not at the dinner table or anywhere,
and Mum might come back one day.
Dad says she won't.
He doesn't say much about her,
which is funny because they
must have been pretty friendly,
don't you reckon,
to get married and all.

I'm not getting married.
I'm not having kids who vomit all over the dinner.
But I might run away from here,
when I'm older.
I might even go look for Mum.

_M_y Dad says ...

My Dad says you're good workers.
He says you're the best he's had in years.
He says he doesn't care what you do in our shed,
as long as you keep working the same.
He said that last night at dinner.
I asked him what you do in our shed,
and Emma laughed.
She hasn't laughed in a while
and then she says,
"Yeah Dad, tell Craig what they're doing."
But Dad doesn't.
He tells Beck not to eat so fast,
probably scared of her vomiting again.
He tells me to mind my own business,
but Dad tells me that at least once a day,
so it's nothing new.
And that's why I'm here now.
So you tell me, OK,
what do you do in our shed here?

Beck talks

My brother Craig,
he thinks he knows everything,
but
he doesn't know who let the dog
wee in his football boots ...

I know.

Screwed

Screwed

I got screwed.
That's how I got pregnant.
Screwed.
If you want to know, I'll tell you.
The truth.
Not what I told Dad.
"My boyfriend, Dad."
The one I made up.
The one who had to leave town with his parents
on account of his father's work.
What a load of bull.
What boyfriend.
We live twenty kilometres from town.
The school bus is our only link.
School buses don't take you anywhere after 3pm.
So one Friday I arranged to stay
at my friend Jenny's place.
The Friday her parents are away,
and we have a party.
All of Year 10.
A big party. A loud party.
And I drink too much,
even dance a bit, just to show myself I can.
I'm drinking away
the twenty kilometres of loneliness out here.
I'm drinking away

the exam results that don't take me anywhere.
I'm drinking away
my clothes that smell of this farm.
I'm drinking away
apples, apple pie, baked apples, apple juice,
apple jam for God's sake.
Then I pass out,
feeling pretty good really.

I passed out on Jenny's lounge.
In the morning I woke on her parent's bed,
with no clothes on.

I got screwed.
I got pregnant.
And I didn't even get to enjoy
becoming this big and ugly.
And nobody in Year 10 knows a thing.
Nobody, that is,
except one person.

School photos

I've been going through my school photos.
Every one since Year 5.
I'm making a list of each boy's features.
Big nose, blond hair, freckles, ears that stick out.
I've got twenty-one boys from Year 10
going back for years.
What a bunch of uglies,
and watching them get uglier every year
are all my girlfriends.
The girls who didn't see anything at Jenny's party.
None of them wear glasses,
so maybe they were just blind drunk.
Blind drunk. Or too scared to remember anything.
Twenty-one boys. Twenty-one prospective fathers.
Ten with blond hair.
Ten with dark hair.
And nerdy Phillip Montain with
red hair, freckles, and … surely not!

It may take years of comparing their features
with that of my baby,
but when I do,
and I know,
well,
someone's going to get screwed,
and, this time,
it won't be me.

Colours

It's the sky I love.
Annabel and I sunbathe
on the hardwood landing of the channel.
I spend hours lost
in the deep summer blue
that goes forever.
I remember being a kid,
me and Dad climbing
onto our roof and looking up.
I'd dream we were flying
and all summer
I'd never want to land.
Annabel and I imagine
animals in the clouds, like kids do,
as a distant jet
writes across the sky
longer than history
and I lay back
remember being a kid again
lost in the innocent colours
of childhood.

Annabel and babies

I think about babies.
My baby, when and if.
Emma's baby, twenty kilometres from town,
no Dad, but lots of apple mush for food.
Jack and me with a baby.
I'm not serious,
I'm just thinking,
passing this Saturday while Jack works
on our car that goes nowhere, but goes nowhere well.
When I left school and got into Uni
I thought my life was made.
Uni, job, money, Jack, travel, house,
Jack, more travel,
and still Jack.
Jack was the constant.

Then one weekend he says
he's quitting.
He wants to drive, anywhere,
as long as it's away from Uni and home.
He wants me to come.
That night my room seemed so small
like a kids room, full of toys and stuff
and none of it meant anything.
I picked up my textbooks
and tried reading them,

and I realised for five years
I'd been reading books that didn't make sense,
and now, I had four more years of it.

I went downstairs and told Mum and Dad.
It's one Sunday they won't forget.
Dad raved, Mum cried.
Then Dad asked *why*?
And all I could answer was
    because I'm too young to decorate a home
    because text books have really bad covers
    because I don't want to wear neat clothes
       and wake every morning at 7.30
    because Jack and I have never been wrong yet
and because I want a year for myself, not my future.

So, late Sunday, we did a deal.
My Dad, the solicitor, bargained
a year off, a deferment,
then back to the books.
I agreed. What else could I do?
And now,
I'm thinking about babies.
Emma's baby.
Jack and my baby.
Growing in my mind, if not in my womb.

The dew-wet grass

The best time is early morning
with the dew-wet grass,
the hills shouldered in mist,
everything quiet.
Annabel and I climb each ladder,
pick a cold apple
and crunch away.
The juice so sharp and tart
it hurts my teeth.
We sit like this,
watching the crows in the fir trees,
the silver-eyes darting among the fruit,
listening for George's tractor
with the empty bins rattling,
calling to be filled.
Annabel, the mist, a farm apple, the birds,
and an orchard waking up.

Lucky Emma

Sometimes
I feel like someone
who's won the smallest prize in the lottery
but lost the ticket.
I think of all the Year 10 boys.
Mark Spencer with his long hair,
black silverchair T-shirt,
leaning back in his chair
playing air-guitar all through Maths.
Peter Borovski and his love affair with himself.
> "Hey Peter, who you sleeping with tonight?
> You're kidding. Yourself again.
> What I'd give for your luck.
> And confidence. And stupidity."
Luke Banfield, who once this year talked to a girl,
yeah, once. He asked her if she'd seen his basketball.
I was that lucky girl.
Or maybe, just maybe,
Steve Dimitri, one of the few fifteen year olds I know
who can eat with his mouth closed
who doesn't know how to play basketball
who doesn't look at the ground when talking to a girl
and who doesn't vomit after three drinks.
He vomits after five drinks …

Actually, I take back what I said.
I feel like someone
who's won the smallest prize in the lottery,
found the ticket
and has to collect the winnings
even though
she doesn't want them.

Emma

I wish I had a boyfriend like you.
Someone who wanted to be with me,
all the time.
It's true.
I watch you two in the orchard.
Every ten minutes he stops picking
to look where you are.
Sometimes you see him, sometimes not,
but he's there, checking you out.
He's not my physical type mind,
but,
I'd love to have someone like that.
And someone to sleep with.
What's that like?
Every night. Does he hold you?
Does he snore?
Does he kiss you before sleep?
God! I've been watching too many soap operas,
but I'd like to know.
The only person I've slept with
is bloody Craig when he was scared one night.
He spent all night dropping silent bombers
under the blankets. What a brother!
Yeah, I'd like a boyfriend,
but I don't like my chances at the moment.
You're a lucky girl,
you know that.

*A*nnabel

It hurt,
listening to Emma talk like that.
It's like some bad dream,
pregnant,
and she didn't even have sex,
well, not really.
It's not the Immaculate Conception though.

I like her.
She's upfront.
She's taking it better than I would.
I'd buy a gun and shoot all twenty-one boys, on suspicion.
And then Jack and I come along,
making love every night in her shed,
and she notices stuff, about Jack.
I've stopped noticing.
She makes me grateful.
I'm going to drive into town later
and buy Jack something,
a CD, or a new shirt maybe.
I might buy Emma
a dress, normal-size,
for after the baby.
A new dress to show the world
on her one trip to town every month.
Her one trip to town, for groceries.

*E*mma and her Mum

Mum and I were cooking
the Sunday before she left.
She stopped blending, and sifting,
she looked out the window
at the day
and I remember it was hot
with not a breath of wind.
Craig and Beck were outside
fighting over whose turn it was
to ride the bike.
Mum looked out, past them,
past the sagging fence,
and the tree-line,
and she said,
"A farm takes a lot out of you,
  sometimes too much."
I thought she was just complaining,
or dreaming,
so I didn't question her.
And that night
Beck vomited all over the Sunday dinner.
That was our last meal together.

When I think of Mum and what she did
I get stiff in this chair
and I look out the same window,

past the same fence, over the same tree-line,
and I touch my stomach
and I whisper,
"I won't ever leave you
  I won't ever …"

Lucky

George thinks we're mad.
Emma thinks we're mad.
Craig and Beck think it's cool
sleeping on a bed of haybales
five metres from the ground
a thin foam mattress
to cover the hay
and blankets, lots of them
piled up high.
Annabel and I climb
the haybale stairs
and feel like King and Queen.
Sometimes we hear the possums
scurrying across the roof
and the birds nesting
in the rusted gutters
and late at night
when the farm sleeps
I hear Annabel's breathing,
a distant owl, and the
slow rhythm of the
windvane on the farmhouse roof.
George and Emma are wrong.
We're not mad, we're lucky.

*G*eorge

George talks about the weather,
he talks about apples,
sometimes, when he's in a good mood,
he talks about his kids.
This is one of those times.
Lunch in the orchard.
Packed sandwiches and a thermos of tea.
Annabel and I sit against the tractor.
George squats in the shade of a tree
and talks,
"Good kids, all of them.
Sure Craig never shuts up,
but what ten-year-old does?
And he's strong.
He helps out around the place.
He'll try and lift anything.
Poor kid will have a hernia before he's a teenager!
And Beck's sweet. She always calls me Dadda.
And I feel like a real Dad when I read to her at night.
She won't sleep without one story, at least.
She's quiet, like me, but smarter.
And Emma, angry with the world.
You can see it, can't you?
But then, she's got reason to be."

George's voice trails off.
We both keep quiet.
He'll tell us if he wants.
"When she first told me,
I wanted to get my gun.
Yeah, I know,
just what you'd expect from a father.
And I would have,
if her mother was around.
I would have made a big show of being angry,
shouted, stormed around looking for bullets,
vowing to chase the kid out of town.
But without Emma's mother here
it seemed pointless.
So I sat and talked, and listened too.
I'm glad I did.
She dismissed the boy, whoever it was.
Someone who's left town.
Some boyfriend I never knew.
You know, I'm still not sure
if she's telling me the truth,
or if she's protecting somebody,
but, it doesn't matter.
What matters is the kid.
I keep telling myself that.
I don't think of becoming a grandad.

I just think of my little girl
becoming a Mum.
Sometimes I wish her mother was here,
for the baby. For Emma.
Not for me.
Emma's mother is dead for me.
She died the day she left."

George looks at us,
as if he's just noticed we're here.
I'm sure he'd been working all that stuff
through these last few months,
here in the orchard,
and it's finally out.

"I talk too much.
She's not dead.
But I'm glad of one thing.
When she left, I'm glad she took her clothes,
her jewellery, even most of the money,
and, by Christ,
I'm glad she left me the kids.
I'd be lost without them.
Lost and bitter.
With them here, I'm only bitter."

George gets up,
tips the tea out under a tree,
packs the esky with what's left
and says,
"Come on, the apples won't pick themselves.
You two are good workers.
I hope you'll stay for the season.
You'll see Emma's baby too, maybe.
By the way, have you ever seen a baby being born?"

Now that was something for Annabel and me
to think of all afternoon.

Like a drunk ...

The night of the day
George told us about seeing the baby
Annabel and I got drunk.
We sat on our favourite haybales
and drank beer, cold and bitter
straight from the bottle.
As the evening light dimmed
we climbed into our makeshift bed
and made noisy love,
like farm animals in the barn
like a drunk falling into a pub, penniless
like a bird caught in the crosshair of a gun
like a truck with no brakes, half-way down a hill
like a kid with a match and a paddock of dry grass
like George without a wife
like Emma without a lover
like a baby, crying to be born.

*E*mma and the memory

Sometimes,
I think I can feel it happening.
I mean,
I can remember how it felt.
It wasn't the pain,
not real pain, like when you cut your hand,
or tread on a rusty nail, or anything,
more an irritation,
a dull irritation,
pressing on me.
And I can smell it too,
like dirty socks left in the laundry basket too long,
and stale beer, but that was probably me.
And I can taste salt, my own tears?
I wasn't crying surely? I was passed out!
Maybe he was crying, the bastard.
I hope he was. Crying with shame.
The only woman he could get was unconscious.
The thought gives me pleasure, at least.
That's all.
I lie in bed, thinking of how it felt.
Not knowing if it's my imagination,
or suppressed memory,
or what really happened.

I remember waking up.
I walked into Jenny's bathroom and vomited.
Only then did I realise I was naked.
Naked, sore, wet, sticky,
and slowly becoming
very, very
suspicious.

Staying at school

Dad says I should have stayed at school,
should have kept going right up to the day.
Now wouldn't that be a sight,
me in a school uniform.
Size 18 wouldn't even fit this belly.
And Personal Development classes
would have had special meaning, don't you think.
Me, six months pregnant,
learning about the correct use of condoms
and other devices,
and you know what I would have said
to that Mrs Barber, our teacher,
as she was showing us condoms on carrots?
I would have put my hand up right there,
and said,
"Miss, how do you keep from getting pregnant
  when you're passed out drunk
  and someone takes advantage?"
It would almost be worth going back to school
just to ask that one question …

*E*mma's dream

Sometimes, when I'm asleep,
I have a dream where
I'm living in a city,
going to work in fancy clothes,
and I have a boyfriend,
and a house of my own
on a normal city street,
you know,
with neighbours, and a shop down the road,
and the only animal is a pet dog,
and the only trees are for shade,
or flowers, or decoration.
In this dream
I go out to the movies
with my boyfriend
and we eat dinner
in a restaurant,
and on weekends I don't have to do anything
but enjoy myself.
And in this dream
I'm walking to work on Monday
and I'm nearly there,
and I remember the baby,
my baby,
and it gets kind of strange
in my dream

because I'm standing outside my work
trying to remember
if I have a baby
or not,
and where it is,
and that's when
I'm not sure
if my dream
is a dream,
or a nightmare.

*S*unday Annabel

Another Sunday of sunshine,
no work, and swimming in the channel.
Emma sits by the bank
watching Jack swing from the rope
and drop into a welcome of still water.
I'm lying here, soaking up a day off,
listening to the sound of nothing
but Jack being a kid again.
Emma talks about school,
and her days on this farm
and how she wants to leave
and every time she mentions leaving
I notice her hands touching her stomach.
I listen and silently vow
to not mention Jack and I leaving
as soon as the work's done.
I tell Emma about where we live
in the suburbs
and the sounds we hear
and the neighbours,
and how Jack and I
just had to get out,
to end up here.
Emma looks up quick when I say this,
and I know what she's thinking.
She knows we can leave when we want.

At that moment Jack falls between us
and starts shaking the water off himself,
like a mad dog,
looking for some attention.

*R*ich, smart, or stupid

You must be rich, smart,
or real stupid you two.
That's what Emma says.
She says only way you could be doing this
is to be rich, smart, or stupid.
She says most people would have to stay home,
study, or work, or have babies maybe.
She says you two get to drive around the place,
work when you want —
she thinks that makes you smart.
And you don't worry about money.
You buy beer whenever,
you buy each other presents,
you go into town and eat —
she thinks that makes you rich.
She says you're rich and smart
but
she says
you're staying here by choice
when you could drive away.
You're staying here working in the orchard,
and sleeping in a shed.
She says that makes you stupid.

A Place Like This

Annabel dreams

It comes in the late afternoon.
I'm in the orchard,
halfway up the ladder,
my neck aching with the weight of the bag
stretching to reach one full red apple,
and I suddenly think of University.

> The afternoon lecture,
> fifty of us, all dressed in jeans & T-shirts
> taking notes
> searching for the phrase that will guarantee
> good exam results.
> Pages and pages,
> and I'd stop for a second
> to touch my forehead.
> I'd feel the small furrow
> between my eyes,
> deepening, it seems,
> with every afternoon lecture.

I sit on the ladder,
rest the bag on the lower rung
hold that apple, rub it along my cheek,
my forehead, smoothing away my past,
and I take long slow crunching bites
as the afternoon breeze

wakens the silver-eyes in the branches,
and I spend all my education
on doing nothing but eating and watching
for just long enough
to feel clean again.

Jack

We came here for the money.
George happened along at the right time.
We had no petrol, nowhere to stay,
and no plans.
When I think about it we had to say yes.
It was that, or go home,
with nothing.
I keep feeling I owe George,
and his children.
I know about the quiet revolution
in every family.
I think of my sister and me eight years ago,
waiting, knowing our Mum was going to die.
Knowing, even at our age.
It took me years to work out what to think,
where to put that stuff.
And I look at Emma here,
and George, the strain in his eyes,
and his voice.
I know where it's coming from
and it won't go away, not for awhile.
I'm glad we came here.
I work extra hard in the orchard,
not for the money anymore,
but for something I can't explain.
Something worth more than money.

The Department lady

I got a visitor from town yesterday,
the Department lady.
Talking about after the baby's born.
What I can get to help.
Money? Not enough.
Health Care. "Don't worry, he won't get sick," I said.
And New Mothers' Monday meeting
where everyone talks about
how beautiful their baby is.
I put a stop to that one.
I asked her if the Department would give me a car,
you know,
to make the meeting on time.
Then she asked me about school.
If I wanted to go back.
I could get money.
I could get my Leaving Certificate.

I wanted to ask her about it,
but she was such a cow.

She started packing up.
Her visit over. The government's job done.
And I didn't like her.
The way she looked at the old lino in the kitchen,
and the dirty dishes,

and she never looked me in the eye,
she looked at her paperwork,
then at our cheap living,
and she asked too many questions.

So when she said goodbye,
I said there was one thing she could do,
I looked at her straight,
the way I'm looking at you now,
and I said,
"You could find out who the father is,
  that'd be a big help ..."

She didn't have an answer for that.
People like her only ever have questions.

Annabel on love

Mine was Year 10.
Jack.
After the movies, at my doorstep,
like a stupid Romance novel.
He kissed me. Nice, but quick.
From my bedroom window
I saw him walking home
and I wanted more.
More was months later.

What can I say?
It's embarrassing now to remember.
He felt heavy and awkward,
lying on top of me.
I'm trying to kiss him,
but his mind's elsewhere.
He's trying to put it in,
and he can't,
so I reached down
and did it for him, simple.

And do you know what was the best bit?
Afterwards.
When he lay in me, limp,
and we held each other,
and started kissing again,

slow and soft, no pressure,
and we started giggling
and kissing still
and touching each other,
relieved it was over,
so now we could start
to really make love,

and we haven't stopped.

*E*mma replies

In Year 9 I kissed a boy,
after school.
Netball training cancelled,
and me alone, shooting hoops,
with an hour to spare, waiting for Dad.
And Rick Harvey comes over,
starts shooting with me.
Offers me a game of keyring,
twenty cents a basket,
and he wins a few,
I win a few.
He owes me forty cents,
when I know he's got no money
or no desire to give me money,
but he's all right
and we sit against the clubhouse
close enough,
and he leans over and starts kissing me.
No questions, no waiting,
and it's OK
so I kiss back.
For a while we just sit there,
our lips pressing,
then I feel his hand
on my leg
tracing a path up

and he's soft and gentle really
so I let him touch me,
you know, there,
outside my pants,
then inside,
and he's not pushy or anything,
and we're both very quiet now,
we've stopped kissing really,
our lips are just together,
our minds are down below, up my dress,
and he puts his finger inside me
and I like it,
and he keeps touching me
inside and out
and soon all I'm thinking of is my body.
I'm hardly sure he's there,
it's me and my body
and I don't move a muscle
in case it all stops
and he keeps doing the same thing
for minutes, for hours
for God knows.
I loved it.
I tell you
it was Christmas, and Easter,
and chocolate cake, and dreams,

and birthdays
and it wasn't Rick Harvey

it was me.
Me and my body,
waking up.

*H*e asks

A funny thing happened today.
In town.
I was in Penney's Department store,
looking at baby clothes,
but daydreaming really.
Thinking how am I going to learn
to be a good mum.
You know, stuff like what to feed him,
or her,
what to do if they look sick,
or hot, or cold, or they cry too much.
I'm thinking all this
as I look through the baby clothes I can't afford
when someone behind me says hello.
It's Adam Barlow, from school. Year 10.
He's in his uniform,
shirt hanging out as usual
socks down, bunched over his sneakers.
He looks nervous,
here in the baby section of Penney's.
He asks how I've been.
He asks how long before the baby's born.
He asks what it's like on the farm
        with no school to worry.
He asks if I know what I'll call it.
He asks what my Dad thinks.

He asks if I'll come back to school afterwards.
He asks again how I've been.
Then he says he's got to go.
He asks far too many questions,
and he answers none.

A gentle kick

As Adam Barlow
walked out of Penney's yesterday
I felt my baby kick.
A gentle tap really,
as if my child
was reminding me
of what's important
and what's not
as Adam Barlow
walked out.

Jack's plans

This is not what I planned.
I wanted lonely beaches with Annabel
and bush camping
beside a river
and maybe even time in the snow
working for a season
amongst the wealthy.
Not here,
jump-starting tractors
sleeping in a shed
working ten-hour days
and now, get this,
going to birth classes
with Emma and Annabel!
I'm eighteen years old
and going to birth classes
for a girl who's not my girlfriend
for a baby that's not mine
and I've got to admit
yes
when I think about it
I've got to admit
I'm looking forward to it!

Emma deserves help,
like George needed help with picking.

And one day,
maybe one day,
Annabel and I will want a baby.
God!
I'm starting to sound like my Dad.
Birth classes.
God!
I hope I don't have to touch anything.
Or lay on my back and breathe funny …

*U*ncle Craig

I hope Emma has the baby at home.
I want to see it,
you know,
being born.
I've seen calves, and lambs,
and even a piglet being born,
but never a real baby.
I reckon it'll be unreal.
Emma says after I was born
I cried for days.
She said I'd never shut up
which is funny really
because Dad says I never shut up now
so maybe that's what happens,
you get born and act the same
your whole life.
Anyway, I'm being real nice to Emma now,
so she'll let me watch
and you know
it means I'll be an uncle,
at my age.
It'll be unreal.

Different

You two are different.
Different than my school friends.
They want to know about the baby, sure,
but only because they're not pregnant
and only because they've got nothing else to say,
not since Jenny's party anyway.
They don't want to know about me.
And how it feels
        to be carrying this great weight
        to be a mother without a boyfriend
        to be missing school, and parties,
        and all of my friends.

I'm glad you're here.
I'm glad you're coming with me to my classes.
I couldn't go alone,
and I need to know stuff
        about the birth.
Truth is, I'm scared.
I'm sure Dad's truck won't start.
Or the ambulance won't come.
Or the midwife.
Or I'll be home alone
with everyone in the orchard.
And the pain,
and how long it'll take.

It's kind of funny really.
Jenny, Peter, Rick Harvey,
even Adam bloody Barlow
are hard at it studying
for their exams
and I'm here
about to study
for something much bigger …
I hope I pass.

Saturday night

The drunk night.
George in town.
The farmhouse asleep.
Annabel and me on the haybales,
stacked high.
We can almost touch the roof.
A bottle of wine,
a dozen beers,
and all night.
Drinking and telling stories,
like
your first embarrassing moment,
the day you learnt Santa wasn't real,
the first time you vomited,
the day you learnt your parents
     did more than just sleep together,
and the first time you got drunk.

Hours of stories,
here, above the farm
on our haybales.

At midnight
Annabel took off all her clothes
     without saying a word,

then asked for another glass of beer, please.
So beautiful, and so well-mannered.

What could I do?
I took a long drink
and undressed.
Annabel cheered
as we stood,
straining to touch the roof,
from our naked haybale world.

The snake

It was two metres long,
brown and mean,
and coming after the chickens.
I nearly stepped on the thing,
and, yes, it was probably as scared as me,
but I jumped higher,
and I picked up the shovel leaning against the shed
and hit it hard,
once, right in the middle,
and again on it's head,
and again and again,
until I was sure,
and again because I'd never be sure,
and then I felt sick
and I ran behind the shed to vomit.
Nothing but green bile came up,
green bile and tears.

I walked back
and George was inspecting it.
A King Brown.
Annabel came out and saw it too.
And Craig. And Beck.
The farm dogs still barked at it,

too late now to be of any use.
Everyone standing out in the sun
looking at the snake,
except Annabel,
who's looking at me.

Annabel's snake

All night, in the shed,
I held Jack.
He was sweating in the chill air,
waking every hour, jerking his legs,
as if running.
I held his arms, tight.
I could feel the muscles tense,
wanting to move,
wanting to flex,
so I held him.
I didn't sleep much, maybe an hour.
Most of the night,
I watched Jack
strike that snake
a thousand times over
and not once, in his sleep,
did that snake die.

*B*eck's snake

After it was all over
I picked it up
took it down to the garden
and I buried it
deep in the ground
where it's quiet
where it's safe
where the dogs can't get it.

Naming rights

I'm going to call him Joseph,
or Josephine if it's a girl.
Why?
Because it's a strong name,
Joe, Joseph.
You give a kid a name like Cameron
or Alfred, or something like that,
and they end up wearing glasses
and looking at computers for the rest of their life.
And Matthew and Nathan
enter school with another
fifteen Matthews and Nathans beside them.
So Joe it is.
He'll turn out strong. Strong and smart.
And I thought of Joseph, you know,
in the Bible.
Him and Mary and Immaculate Conception.
Well, I reckon my baby's conception
was pretty damn immaculate.
And I couldn't call the kid Jesus,
could I?
Joseph.
Josephine.

Cheers

It's six weeks since we left home.
Our great adventure ran out of petrol
and stopped on this farm.
The harvest is nearly done.
George looks happier,
he lets me drive the tractor,
he lets us finish early on Friday.
He even let Emma come to town with us last Saturday.
We watched the local football.
Big farmers tackling even bigger truckies
and their sons, stepping effortlessly
around them all.
A few of Emma's friends came up to say hello.
They all asked the same questions.
Baby this, baby that.
Emma only existed as the baby-carrier it seems.
They all looked slightly guilty,
especially the girls,
as though a bond had been broken,
or something, I don't know.
We sat on the bonnet of our car
and clapped
when someone scored a try,
and we all cheered whenever
Adam Barlow got tackled.
Emma, Annabel, and I
cheered the game,
and cheered ourselves.

*E*mma and apples

I needed to get away from the farm,
if only for a day.
People say apples have no smell,
well, even now,
twenty kilometres away,
I can still smell them.
I'll smell them when I'm dead, I reckon.
If you stay too long on the farm
you'll get the same, for sure.
It's alright for Craig.
He wants to be a farmer,
he's got apple juice for blood.
And Beck? She'll escape
on her brains, I bet.
But me? Where do I fit?
Not on the farm,
not in a one-pub town
like this,
not anywhere I guess.
Maybe in a city,
where I can get lost,
get lost for good.

Emma

After the football on Saturday,
when Jack, Annabel and me
got back into the car,
I had this urge to drive and not stop,
to tell Jack to just keep going,
to follow the Midland Highway forever,
just the three of us.
I've had enough of this town,
and my friends
asking guilty stupid questions,
and I've had enough
of the smell of our farm
and the animals' noise,
and the winter winds whipping down Broken Lookout
and rattling our house.
I wanted to forget being pregnant
and remember being young,
like Jack and Annabel are with each other.

I was thinking all this on Saturday
in the car
when we reached Broken Lookout
where Jack parked, for the view,
and Annabel said,
"There's the farm.
It looks so beautiful at night."

Jack agreed,
and I looked at the stars,
the thousands of stars in the cold sky,
but I couldn't say a single word.

Craig hates school

I hate school.
I hate school.
I hate the kids in Year 8 and 9
who come up to me at lunch
and ask "hey, where's fat Emma.
Where's your sister, we want to try our luck."
I hate school
I can't fight the big kids,
but I do anyway.
I get one good kick, or punch,
before they clobber me,
or the teachers come.
The sooner Emma has a baby, the better.
I hate school.

A place like this

I go walking, early.
Me and my baby.
Me and my big stomach.
We walk to the channel
sit on the bank
watch the dragonflies
like mad helicopters cutting the surface.
I go walking
to avoid the kitchen
and the smell of food,
too early for cooking,
Craig and Beck arguing,
and Dad looking out the window,
thinking of money.
I go walking to watch the trees
and the sun's light filtering through them.
I talk to my baby.
I describe the farm.
I tell him about the apples
and the blossoms in spring
and the Paterson's Curse that covers the hills
and the birds gorging on rotten fruit.
I tell him everything
as we walk.
Maybe so he won't be disappointed
being born into
a place like this.

Weird

Weird

It's weird.
Very weird.
I started going to birth classes
with Emma and Jack.
I sat in the room, on the floor,
beside them.
Ten couples and the three of us.
Eleven couples holding hands, and me,
not knowing whether to touch Emma or Jack.
And Jack's weird,
he looks at me when he talks to Emma
and looks away.
He can't focus.
He's not sure who he's partner to.
He wants to help Emma I know,
so do I.
But I can't help there.
I can't be her partner,
neither can Jack,
not with me around.
So I keep away.
I stay here in the shed.
I think about Emma's baby,
and Jack.
And where Jack and I are going,

which is nowhere it seems,
and it's all too weird,
too weird to work out.

Craig and the cows

Hey, you know what?
Some Year 9 kids have painted the cows.
Farmer Austin's best dairy cows.
Each cow has a red number on its side.
Some even have sponsors!
One's sponsored by Nike!
Number 23. The Shane Warne of dairy cows!
It's all round school.
It's all round town.
There's even a photo in the newspaper,
old man Austin shaking his head,
looking at his stupid cows.
Everyone at school reckons he should
leave it on, and call them by number,
    "Number 12, your turn for milking."
    "Number 8, stop scratching against the gum tree."
Our footy coach says we should adopt one,
as a mascot.
He says we play like a bunch of cows anyway.
It's great.
The town hasn't been so happy in years.
It's great.
All over a herd of painted cows!

Annabel is ready

I'm ready.
The work is nearly done.
I want to move.
I can almost smell the road
and hear the soft hum of tyres
rolling through this year
where Jack and I plan nothing.
I'm ready. I know.

But Jack's dreaming.
He sits against the shed
reading the same page of his book
over and over.
He's looking for a reason to go,
or stay.
He walks through the house of his past,
hoping he'll find the right door,
hoping he'll find the key.

It pisses me off.
I want to go and shake him,
shake that house down.
I want to tell him he's in the wrong house,
at the wrong time.
I want to tell him we've built a new one,
with no doors locked,

no keys,
just him and me and open space.

I want to move.
Even if it's back to
sleeping in the car by the highway
with tinned food for dinner.
I don't care.
I'm ready.

Jack and the beach

The work is nearly done.
Once the top orchard is stripped,
we're finished.
A week, maybe two.
We've saved enough money
for six months of holiday,
camping on a beach.
I keep thinking of the one
I went to as a kid,
with Mum and Dad kissing on a towel
and my sister at the shop, talking to boys.
I want to do nothing for a long time.
No more apples,
or 7am starts.
Annabel and me.
Open fires, books to read,
bathe in the creek behind the surf,
and enough petrol in the car
to go to town whenever we want.
Annabel and me
at the beach.
And we'll get there,
we will,
after the baby.

Annabel

Jack's mad!
He thinks Emma and the baby
are his responsibility.
Uncle Jack.
Mad Uncle Jack.
He's like some crazy social worker.
Everything he touches he can fix.
I should remind him of the car!
So, what's he going to do?
Help Emma have the baby,
and then what?
Jack can't save the world,
beginning on this farm.
This is Emma's life,
she'll work it out.
Jack's got to leave it,
leave it to Emma,
and George.
They'll work it out.
Of that I'm sure.

Making sense

My Mother died when I was ten.
The last time we spoke
was late in the afternoon,
after school.
She was in bed, resting,
trying to read,
and it was a beautiful day.
The sun shone right up to her bed
and she told me stories,
as well as she could —
she was heavily drugged for the pain.
And I told stories right back.
Only my stories were ones in the future.
What I planned to do.
Me and Dad and my sister.
I told her
to make her know we'd stay together,
you know, afterwards.
I didn't have a clue
what would really happen,
but I kept talking.
And one story was about grandkids.
About me and a wife and babies.
I did it for her.
I didn't want kids, I was ten years old!
I wanted my Mother, alive, and healthy.

But I made up this story,
and Mum smiled and listened,
she even laughed when I promised her
a football team of grandkids.
Then her laughing turned to coughing
and that awful sound she couldn't break.
I left her to rest.
I kissed her forehead,
the way she kissed me every night, before bed,
and I closed the door.
The sun still shone brightly …

And that's why I go to birth classes with Emma,
why I feel I can't leave now.
Maybe it doesn't make sense.
It's like a death.
Or a birth.

Annabel and the car

Last night
I got in our car
and drove.
Just me.
No Jack. No Emma.
I drove along Turpentine Road,
up to the quarry.
I parked, turned the radio up loud,
and lay back.

I figured I had two choices.
I could keep driving and not come back.
Jack can have the money, and the beach,
and whatever else he can invent.
I'd leave the car outside his house,
and go back to my life.

My other choice was to say *no* to Jack.
To simply say *no*.
The baby will be born,
with or without him here.
And Emma will be a good mother,
and there's George, and Craig, and quiet Beck.

Lots of children don't have fathers,
or mothers.
Jack should know that,
more than all of us.

Craig

Emma says
her son's not living on a farm
all his life
and he's not picking apples
or praying for rain
or busting a gut fixing things that
can't be fixed
and he's not
wearing the same shoes winter and summer
cause that's all he's got.
And Emma says
if it's a girl
she's not marrying a farmer
or cooking all day
for kids who vomit it all back up
and she's not spending nights
watching TV and dreaming,
or getting pregnant at sixteen
and looking after brothers and sisters
and fathers and family.
Emma says all this
and I'm thinking this baby
better be born soon
because it's got a lot of living to do
and a lot of learning on what
not to do.

Birth classes

Ten farmers in flannelette shirts
and me
sit on our knees in a circle
at the CWA Hall.
Ten farmers' wives lean back
against their husbands.
Emma leans against me.
I hold her hands in mine
and talk quietly,
repeating the Instructor's words.
Sometimes I add my own.
Silly stuff like
"she'll write books
  she'll call you Mum, and me Uncle Jack
  she'll grow up smart.
  He'll grow up smart
  he'll never pick apples."
I just talk away.
Emma holds my hand tighter,
offering me encouragement.
I don't care what the farmers think.
I hold Emma's hands and talk.
We both close our eyes,
and listen.

The perfect sky

I stop the car
a few kilometres from the farm,
at Broken Lookout.
Emma and I sit on the warm bonnet
and look at the distant farm lights.
We don't say much.
Birth classes take it all.
I tell Emma about my Mother.
Dead. Eight years now.
I tell her how I remember everything about her.
Her hair, her soft voice in the dark,
her way of looking at my sister and me.
I tell Emma I'll never forget a thing.
Not because my Mum's dead.
Not because I miss her.
But because she's my Mum
and it's important.
And before she died,
she taught me that.
She taught me what's important,
and what isn't.
And I've never forgotten.
And that's what mothers do, I say.
We look at the lights some more
under the perfect sky.
I try to remember every detail
of what's important.

Annabel and George

Jack and Emma were at birth classes last night.
I was in the shed, again.
Reading. Dreaming really,
of the beach,
of the world away from apples.
And George knocks at the door of his own shed.
He wants to talk.

He's worried Emma will leave, after the baby.
After we go.
She'll leave this farm, this land,
and him, and Craig, and Beck,
and home.
George is scared.
His voice is tight, his eyes darting.

I tell him to wait.
I tell him to look at Emma
and how she walks
and how she holds her stomach when she walks
as if she's protecting the child
as if she's afraid to let something precious fall.

I tell George to trust his daughter
and her hands.
I tell him those hands won't fail.
And I pray I'm right.

Annabel

After George left
I couldn't read anymore.
I sat on the haybales
and tried to work things out.
But all I could think was that
I felt like an intruder,
here on the farm.
For weeks we'd been helpers.
When George couldn't get pickers,
we worked.
When Emma needed someone for classes,
we volunteered.
But now,
with George wandering his farm,
like a lost man,
waiting for Emma and Jack to come home,
I knew.
We were intruding.
It was all too private.
Maybe we were wrong,
wrong to offer with the classes,
I'm not sure.
Only now, maybe,
they needed each other,
not us.

Craig and his mad dad

I think Dad's going mad!
True.
Last night I saw him
wandering around the house
in his overalls and slippers.
It was a full moon
so I could see good
and you know what they say
about a full moon — it makes you mad!
Well, Dad's walking around the yard,
and he wanders out to the orchard.
He picks an apple,
a big juicy apple,
and I think,
fine, he's going to eat it.
But no.
He starts tossing it in the air,
higher and higher
and he catches it every time.
Now Dad hardly ever throws balls
and never but never throws apples.
He's always telling me
not to drop them into the bin
in case they bruise,
and here he is, a full moon,
playing catch with an apple.

Very weird.
He's out in the orchard forever it seems,
just walking around,
with this apple,
tossing it from one hand to the other.
And this is the best bit —
he walks back to the house
and he looks up
and sees me at the window.
I'm thinking I'm going to get it
for being up so late,
but all he does is cup his hands,
like this,
meaning he wants me to catch the apple.
So I lean right out the window
and Dad throws it, perfect!
I catch it with both hands.
I take a big crunchy bite
and Dad smiles
and waves goodnight.

It was a good apple too.
A good apple, picked by a madman,
on a full moon night.

Craig and cricket

At school today,
Sports Day,
we had our cricket final
against Blairthorn School.
Most of the school were there,
you know,
cheering us on.
I got out for a duck.
I lifted my head, as usual,
and got clean bowled.
But when Blairthorn were batting,
and it was getting tight,
their best batsmen
hit this huge shot
and it was going for four, or maybe six,
and I ran around the boundary,
dived full-length, sideways,
and caught it!
Everyone cheered,
and my duck was forgotten,
and now we stood a chance of winning.

It was a good catch,
my second good catch in 24 hours,
don't you reckon?

*E*mma and the right way

I've been thinking hard.
It's all I can do right now.
Think. And wait.

I needed Jack and Annabel
on this farm two months ago.
They came out of nowhere,
and gave me hope.
The way they were, together.
Everything they do is positive.
They're not like the kids at school.
I needed them.
I needed help with birth classes.
But now,
I've been thinking about Dad.
I've never thought about him.
He just was.
I worried about Mum, wherever she is.
I worried about Beck and Craig, without Mum.

But Dad, look at him.
Three children, no wife,
a farm that barely pays
and he gets up every morning
sits on the veranda
watching the sunrise

and he counts himself lucky.
And when I come home pregnant
he doesn't yell, or rant, or blame.
He just keeps on going.
He looks almost proud of me.
Now he worries I'll leave.
He worries Jack and Annabel leaving
will mean I'll follow,
maybe not after them, but away,
anywhere.
But he's not saying anything.
He's going to let me choose,
I know.
It's his way.
It's the right way.

G*uts*

Maybe I don't have the guts to leave.
It shouldn't be too hard.
Mum left.
She packed and was gone in a day.
Vanished.
I could do that,
only I'd write, and phone,
and maybe come back,
you know, later.
A girl, pregnant or not,
could get lost in the city.
And it couldn't be worse than here,
could it?
Bloody Mum. I hate her.
I hate her for going so easy.
For going and staying away.
Craig and Emma still hope she'll come back,
someday.

I can see it now.
I leave home
   for the city
   I'm walking down the street
   and guess who's walking towards me
   and what do I say to her
   "hello Mum"

or
    "hello Grandma."
Now that would be funny.
So funny I'd have to stop myself
from hitting her,
from telling her what I really think,
but maybe I don't have the guts
for that either.
But when I look at this farm
I keep thinking
it's not whether I have the guts to go
but
if I have the guts to stay.

*E*mma and leaving

Last night
Jack told me about the beach,
and his plans,
and the more he talked,
the more nervous I got.
I don't know why.
I can't tell.

I just listened.
I listened and dreamed.

And that's what I'm doing now.
I'm dreaming.
Only sometimes it's hard dreaming
when
Beck needs help with her homework
and Craig's talking nonstop
and Dad's burning the dinner
and my own kid's kicking his way around my belly.

So I'm not thinking good
when Beck,
bloody Beck,
she who never says a word,
looks up at me over the pages
and says

"you're smart,
you know that Emma?"

And it all makes sense,
even to smart old Emma.

A Young Orchard

A young orchard

It wasn't what Beck said,
but that she said it at all.
I knew.
I'm staying here.
No dreams of fancy clothes
    and cafes
    and movies
    and working in a sleek office tower.
It was old lino
and peeling paint
and apple pies every dessert
and my baby eating apple mush
and Craig and Beck and Dad.
But it was more than that,
it was me.
Me without Jack and Annabel
and some excuse to leave.
Me without Mum and the fear
of loneliness and boredom.
Me, making my way.
And Joseph, or Josephine.
Me, back at school.
Me, taking that bloody bus
    the twenty kilometres
    and the baby in childcare

while I study hard,
harder than ever before.
And me getting out of here,
my way,
when I'm ready,
with my child.
Me, getting out but
not like Mum,
running so fast
she's too scared to look back.
Me, getting out but
being able to come back.
Me and my home.
Me and the baby,
happy in the orchard
picking those stupid apples
if we choose.
Or me and my baby
leaving
finding another orchard
a young orchard
and making it ours.

Annabel

When we first came here
Jack and I had a picnic every Sunday.
We went to the channel
or across town to Brown Creek.
We lay on the blanket in the sun,
and slept. Or drank a few bottles,
and dived into the chill water.

Today we asked Emma along
and she said no.
She said no in a strange way,
and I think I know what she meant.

Here at Brown Creek
I lean over and pick up a few rocks.
I aim for a boulder on the far side of the creek.
I say to myself, as Jack sleeps,
if the first one hits
we leave this week
and drive, non-stop, to the beach.

I choose the biggest rock
and let rip,
and my aim is true.

ow

Jack wakes,
and I tell him of the boulder
and my perfect aim.

I tell him I've decided,
we leave this week.
We fill the car with petrol now,
just to be sure.

I tell him I'm not angry,
or crazy.
I tell him I'm ready,
and he should be too.
I tell him to think of our two years together.
Think of us leaving Uni and ending up here.
Think of us making love on a stack of haybales.
Think of the mornings in the orchard
and the taste of dew-fresh apples.
Think of him and me and Emma at birth classes.
Think of Craig and his painted cows.
Think of Emma here on the farm
and the rich soil of family.

And it makes sense, I know.
I hit the boulder with one throw,
and it made a strong ringing sound,
that echoed back across the creek.
We're leaving.

*E*mma and her Dad

Jack and Annabel
have filled their car with petrol, at last,
and gone on a Sunday drive.
A picnic, like young lovers.
They asked me along.
I said no.
I said, stay young lovers together,
and they looked at me funny.

Dad's working on the tractor, again.
Beck and Craig are in the treehouse,
playing quiet, for a change.
I take Dad some tea,
and this cake I made,
which wouldn't win any prizes
but it's OK —
I don't want to be a cook or anything.

Me and Dad sit by the tractor,
the dogs hang around for food
and the afternoon settles
on an orchard stripped of fruit.
The season is over.
Jack and Annabel can go whenever they like.
They've been waiting,
the whole farm's been waiting,
waiting for me to have this baby.

I start talking to Dad
about my baby
about Mum leaving us
and never coming back.
I tell him about school
and the long afternoons in Maths
when I dreamed myself away,
away anywhere.
And about Jack and Annabel,
smart and ready
and I'm wondering where all that smart comes from
and I figure some from parents,
some from school, and some from a place inside you.
I tell Dad
I got smart from him,
and I'm smart deep inside,
but from school I got nothing but pregnant.

I can curse school for that or curse myself,
but what's the point.
So I think school deserves more
and I say to Dad
I want to go back to school
after the baby
and for the first time in a while
Dad looks straight at me

and I'm scared to look back
because I'm not sure what it means
so I keep talking.
I tell him I rang Childcare in town
and I rang the Department
and I know it'll be hard
but it won't cost much
for the baby to be looked after
while I'm in school
and I know I can manage it
maybe even Beck and Craig can help.
I know I can do it
and I keep talking
afraid to look at Dad
and I say
Jack and Annabel should go,
go to their beach,
before the baby, who's taking his own good time.
I'll tell them thanks
and I'll promise an invitation
to the Christening.
I look straight at Dad now
knowing I have to
and he's still looking back.
I tell him when Jack goes

I'll need help with birth classes
and maybe he could come along
and he smiles.
I think it's a Dad smile.
He leans over
and takes another slice of cake
and he keeps smiling
and he says,
calm as you please
"You make a good cake Emma
  a good cake"
and I know everything will be fine,
just fine.
So I reach for a slice
to feed my baby
and myself.
I take a big slice.

A Full Tank

Craig knows

Me and Beck,
we're gunna miss you two.
We reckon you're lucky,
leaving here to spend all your time
on some beach.
Maybe we can visit
on school holidays or something?
You let us know OK?

I'm gunna miss you two.
I like the way you get drunk
every Saturday night
when you think the farm's asleep.
I like the way
you sleep late on Sunday
and stumble out of the shed
like two old drunks.
But most of all I like
the way you spend your nights
up there, on the haybales.

Yeah, that's right,
one night I couldn't sleep
and I came out here, real quiet,
so yeah,
now I know what you do in our shed!

*I*t's time

We've packed the car,
Annabel and me.
I've filled the tank with petrol,
this time, we won't stop.

I wander into the orchard, alone.
I'm looking for the first tree I stripped,
two months back.
I'm sure I'll remember which one.
It was on the end of a line,
the highest on the farm.
The view looked over the valley and the hills,
and all the way to Broken Lookout.
I climb the tree,
and sit for a while.
The rotting fruit covers the grass
and the leaves are starting to drop.
I hear a crow up in the fir trees,
and a semitrailer on the distant highway.
And I can hear my Dad's voice
telling me to go, just go.

I hear Annabel's footsteps,
coming through the grove
and I know
that my world echoes with her sound

and that I should follow it,
the way Emma will follow her baby,
hopeful, and sure,
and tied to this farm
and these people.
I know
that today,
with a full tank,
and with Annabel,
that it's time to go.

Annabel and the orchard

Jack's up some tree.
Dreaming.
I hope the branch breaks
and he lands on his head.
That's how I feel sometimes.
But I'm glad we argued over leaving.
Sometimes you need to make a choice.
Like giving up Uni.
Like coming to this farm to work.
Like Emma getting drunk one night,
waking up pregnant,
and still saying yes to the baby
after all that.
Like me and Jack now, together,
going.
Starting now.
Starting today.
When we leave this orchard.
That is, if I can get my love, the mad bastard,
out of the tree.

Warm

*F*or the sun

It's the first rain of the season.
I think of Jack and Annabel
on some beach. I hope the sun shines there.
I can hear Dad chopping wood,
ready for a long cold spell
with frost on the orchard
cracking under our feet.
The clouds have covered the hills
and the trees are stark winter bones.
I touch my stomach, gently,
feel such power and weight
but if I get any bigger
they'll need a wheelbarrow
to get me to hospital.
I love my baby.
I don't care how it happened.
I don't care how cold this winter gets.
I stand on the veranda
and feel warmer than I've ever felt.
The wind rattles the shed door
to remind me of Jack and Annabel.
I hope they're swimming naked
in clear salty water.
I'm glad they came.
I can see Craig and Beck
walking home from the highway.

Craig's swinging his lunatic school-bag
and Beck's wandering slow, in no hurry.
I sit on the squatter's chair
put my feet up on the veranda railing,
lean back, close my eyes,
and wait, for the sun.

Steven Herrick is one of Australia's most popular poets. He lives in Katoomba in the Blue Mountains in Australia with his wife, Cathie, and their two sons.

I look out the window,
and although it's dark,
the moon
illuminates the scene
as if a faraway
floodlight
is hung
from the sky.

So much whiteness.
Everywhere.

Come back,
angel.

Let us fly
away
from
here.

Also by Lisa Schroeder

From Simon Pulse | Published by Simon & Schuster